THE APPLE-GREEN TRIUMPH

and Other Stories

THE
APPLE-GREEN
TRIUMPH

and Other Stories

MARTHA LACY HALL

Louisiana State University Press

Baton Rouge and London

1990

C. 2

99 98 97 96 95 94 93 92 91 90   5 4 3 2 1
Designer: Albert Crochet
Typeface: Linotron Trump Mediaeval
Typesetter: The Composing Room of Michigan, Inc.
Printer and binder: Thomson-Shore, Inc.

Grateful acknowledgment is made to the editors of the following
publications, in which the stories listed originally appeared:
Sewanee Review (Spring, 1990), "The Mercy of the Lord";
Shenandoah (Spring, 1989), "Miss Robbie's Cup of Tea";
Southern Review (Autumn, 1986; Spring, 1987; Spring, 1988),
"The Birthday Party," "Crab Celestine," "Saturday Job"; *Virginia
Quarterly Review* (Autumn, 1988; Summer, 1990), "The
Authoress," "The Apple-Green Triumph."

LIBRARY OF CONGRESS CATALOGING-IN-PUBLICATION DATA

Hall, Martha Lacy, 1923–
    The apple-green triumph, and other stories / Martha Lacy Hall.
    p.   cm.
    Contents: The apple-green triumph—Elinor and Peggy—Miss
Robbie's cup of tea—The mercy of the Lord—The birthday party
—Saturday job—Crab Celestine—Quicksand—The authoress.
    ISBN 0-8071-1608-4 (alk. paper)
    I. Title.
PS3558.A3716A83   1990
813'.54—dc20   90-5658
                                                     CIP

For Matt, Clay, and Andrew

Contents

The Apple-Green Triumph

BEFORE OPENING the car door, Lucia took a deep breath of the Louisiana night air. She was not unaware of its heaviness, its moistness, the smells of Lake Pontchartrain—salt, seaweed, water creatures, all mixed with the sounds produced by the wind slapping water against the seawall, soughing in the tops of tall pines against a black sky.

She pressed hard on the starter in the old Triumph. It ground, coughed, and was silent. "Oh, my God," she said, and hit the steering wheel with her fist. If it wouldn't start, she would just have to have Everett paged at the New Orleans airport. Tell him to get on a Greyhound bus for Mississippi. He should have done that in the first place or flown into Jackson. "Start!" she growled and pressed again, and it did. She floored the accelerator, in neutral, and the engine roared underfoot, confident and, as always, a little arrogant for so small a tiger. The beam of the headlights crawled across the wall and the screened porch as she slowly backed out of the carport and turned toward the street.

"I'm out of my mind," she said aloud. "I'm just out of my everloving mind." She had begun talking to herself after Chris died two years ago. They had had such a good time talking that when he was no longer there she just kept on talking. "I am my own best company," she sometimes said, picking figs or surveying herself at the full-length mirror, ready to go out. She slowed and looked at her watch under the corner streetlight. Ten o'clock.

"Seventy-five-year-old fool heading to New Orleans at ten o'clock at night." She braked, shifted the gear, and rounded

1

the corner, leaving Lakeshore Drive. "A damn fool." The lights beamed across the spray-painted command on the wall of the high school gym: LADY OF MERCY STOMP HOLY GHOST FRIDAY NIGHT!

Scarcely aware of thunder to the south, she drove slowly, peering intently through her glasses and the flat little windshield. She had decided not to drive at night over a year ago, and she felt that her dear old car might be better able to make it across the twenty-six-mile causeway than she was. "Old cars can be overhauled." As this one had been recently. A big car rushed up to an intersection and slammed to a stop. Startled, she swore.

"Just tell me one thing good about being old. Just one thing!" She simply hadn't felt this way as long as she had Chris. Any woman who claimed she didn't need a strong man didn't know what she was talking about. She drove on toward the causeway, through a tunnel of night-darkened oaks between the streetlights of Ste. Marie, Louisiana. "I just have to do it," she said, tears in her voice. Everett hadn't changed a bit. She hadn't seen him for nearly ten years and never expected him to fly down for Ann's services. And what did he do but call her at nine o'clock tonight out of the blue, from the New Orleans airport.

"Can you pick me up?" he said, like he was down at the Ste. Marie bus depot and it was twenty years ago.

"Do you know how old I am?" she wanted to scream at him.

"Brat. Sixty-year-old brat." He hadn't come for the other funerals—Dora's, Tom's, Margaret's. Not since their parents'. Well, Ann was his twin. Maybe there still was something special there, dormant, come to life at the incident of death. And some burst of confidence and energy had made her say, "I'll pick you up. Just sit tight." The call had given her an illusion of vigor, the big sister again, always there, ready. She had to do it.

When she thought of Ann she began to cry and had to pull

over to the curb and hold her face in a handful of tissues. "I thought I was through crying," she sobbed. "Ann, Ann! I could kill you for leaving me high and dry like this." Then she began to laugh at what she'd said. Ann would have laughed. She took another tissue from the box on the dash and cleaned her glasses and blew her nose. As she drove back onto the wide highway, wind gusts swept overland from the lake, bringing the first raindrops.

"Don't rain! Don't rain!"

By the time she approached the causeway she was in a downpour, windshield wipers working fast and noisily. She pulled up to the toll booth and handed the man a dollar. Reflected lights blurred on the choppy water of Lake Pontchartrain. Red lights and white lights nearby, and far ahead a smoldering luminescence in the low, heavy clouds over New Orleans.

"Bad night to be headin' for Sin City," the man said.

"Mission of mercy," said Lucia, and moved forward, chin high.

Chris's apple-green Triumph was in fine shape for its age. Duffy Peek had just been all over it, spent three days like he and Chris used to do together. She loosened her tight grip on the steering wheel, arthritis grinding out its pain in knobby knuckles, hurting like the devil. For that matter it hurt in her shoulders, neck, back. "Just a dilapidated old bag of bones."

But she could quickly call up one of those lovely healing memories of Chris's voice: "Cut that out, you beautiful babe. You're in great shape, and you look like a million dollars," and she saw that wide smile, white teeth, tanned face. Fine old face. The car seemed more cozy and safe while rain pounded the canvas top, windshield, and danced on the hood.

Then Ann pushed back into Lucia's thoughts. Ann and Everett had been her real-live dolls. She was fifteen when they were born, she was the eldest of six, the tallest, the child-lovingest, the chauffeur, Mother pro tem, Daddy called her.

She adored the twins and simply took them over, rocked two cribs at once, changed diapers, warmed bottles—old-fashioned bottles with rubber nipples that Everett learned to pull off in his crib. Lucia carried them around, baby legs straddling both her hips. She dressed them in their little matching clothes for Myrt to roll them down to the Methodist Church corner in their double stroller, where all the nurses gathered in the afternoons with their charges, little white children fresh from their bathtubs. Ann became her love, and they had remained close for the rest of Ann's life.

"I never could believe she grew up. How did she get to be sixty years old? She barely made that. Why did she have to die before me? Emphysema, like the others. And Daddy. Ann didn't even smoke." Lucia had spent the last months going back and forth between Ste. Marie and Sweet Bay, sitting with Ann at home or in the hospital, at whichever place Ann lay propped up, crowding words between breaths, oxygen tank nearby, plastic tubes in her nostrils. They reviewed their whole lives. "And I made you my executor!" Lucia said, accusingly, and they laughed like fools, as they always had, no matter how bad off Ann was. No matter how hard it was for Lucia. Almost to the end. They weren't together when she died in her sleep.

"I can't believe things are ending this way. I've buried all of them. All but Everett. God knows he'd better outlive me. I'm sick of sitting on the edges of graves in that plot." She would talk to Everett about that, about his place now. Thank God for him. A good dependable younger family member. "Perhaps he will come back home with me for a few days, and we can relax, visit, talk about the future . . ." The wind and rain came on hard from the lake, almost blindingly. She couldn't possibly drive the minimum speed. Traffic was blessedly light.

An enormous white semi was overtaking the green Triumph, fast. "Slow down, idiot." How could he see to drive that fast? The white hulk rumbled past, rocking the small car fearsomely.

She remembered the day Chris drove it into her driveway, a tiny motor-roaring thing, the top down, unfolded his long legs, and rose from the brown leather seat. "Are you Mrs. Collins?" he asked, and his smile was as arresting as his apple-green car.

"I am," said Lucia, removing her gardening gloves and dropping the bamboo rake on the leaf pile. She took hasty note of his appearance, thatch of white hair, rumpled by the wind, plaid well-tailored shirt, good suitably faded jeans, and white deck shoes. He had a newspaper under his arm. He was the boater who had called in answer to her ad.

"My name is Neilson, Chris Neilson. I called about your ad. Let's see, you have a lantern, Coleman stove, rope, fishing tackle. Got an anchor?"

"That and more." She smiled politely.

"May I see them?"

"Certainly. They're right back here in the storeroom. I'll get the key." She fetched the key off the kitchen hook, and Chris Neilson followed her to the dark green door off the carport. She switched on the light. "I have a 50-horsepower motor, some seats, life preservers, quite a few things. Go in and look them over."

He stayed in the storeroom a while. She could tell what he was examining by the familiar sounds of wood, metal, canvas. When he stepped out he smiled again and said, "You all lost interest in boating?"

"My husband died several years ago, and I'm just now getting rid of some of his things."

"I know how that is. Been through it. I'm going to try living on my boat."

"I see. Well, do you see anything you need in there?"

"I surely do. Are those two new deck chairs for sale? I could use them. And the lantern I could use. How about the radio?"

"Any of it or all of it." She reached in her shirt pocket and handed him a typewritten list with prices.

"Good," he said. "Tell you what. I live in New Orleans, but I'll be back in a pickup this afternoon late if that's okay."

"That's fine. I'll be here."

He smiled again and slid into the car.

"You have a—an interesting car. I don't believe I ever saw a sportscar that color."

"Probably not. I had this one painted. Gaudy, isn't it?"

"It's bright . . . springlike," she laughed like he wasn't a stranger. She was the stranger.

After he left she picked up her rake and poked it around in the leaves. What an interesting man. She hadn't noticed an "interesting man" since Henry died. She embarrassed herself.

Lucia realized she was handling the car well despite everything. She felt a ripple of pride in her spine. The Triumph was so small, not even comfortable, really, but she couldn't part with the crazy little thing. First she had sold Chris's pickup, then finally her sedan. Sentiment. What made men love their cars so? She had loved the man, and the car was the most tangible thing she had left of him. "Oh, Chris." She was married to Chris for eight years—a fling and a lark for an old couple. Old in birthdays. She couldn't remember either of them being sick for a day together. "It was more than a fling and a lark."

"You look like a smart woman. What do you do?" he said later when he dropped by with no excuse.

Confronted with such a question, she blurted, "I work like a dog in this house and yard. I make fig and mayhaw preserves and green-tomato pickles. I read a couple of books a week. I 'do' book reviews." She stopped, aghast at her ready biography to a stranger. That was the beginning. He was interested.

Lucia loosened her hurting hands. "What we did was laugh and talk." And live a little. A lot. Like she had not thought possible. For eight years. Sometimes she still found it hard to believe that they had had the good fortune to find each other.

"Right there in your own backyard," he would say and put his arms around her.

One night eating their own catch on the deck of his boat, rocking ever so gently on the Tchefuncte River, he said, "Marry me and come live on my boat."

"Marry you! You want to get legally hitched to a sixty-five-year-old crone?" It was as good as "Yes."

"I want your money."

"My dowry consists of my medicare."

"I'll accept that." More seriously, "So, we're sixty-five years old. Let's see how much fun we can have."

So they were married. By a New Orleans judge they both knew. They lived in her house on the lake, but she became a boat person, too. It was an unruffled transition, becoming a married woman again. Chris was an affectionate man. To her naïve surprise, he was a tender and passionate lover, and to her greater surprise, her pleasure with him was more intense than she had ever known. "You're some woman," Chris would say. And "Back from the dead!" That was lagniappe.

They drove to New Orleans for Saints games at the Superdome and for shows at the Saenger. They dined with friends at home, in the city, and in restaurants around the lake. They cooked on the grill, and they played gin and sipped wine in the evening.

Occasionally Chris would have an extra evening drink or two, on the boat anchored a mile or so from the north shore. He would tell her ribald stories and sing noisily from an endless repertoire of war songs, using his glass for a baton.

Creeping along in the night through wind and rain over Lake Pontchartrain, Lucia shook her head remembering Chris singing one night, "Bless em all! Bless em all! The long and the short and the tall! There'll be no promotions this side of the ocean. So cheer up, my lads, Fuckem all!"

"Hush up, Chris! Your voice carries across this water like you have a microphone." She was interrupted by a baritone from a winking light a quarter mile farther out. "Fuckem all!

Fuckem all! The long and the short . . ." And then they could all hear the laughter bounce over the light chop and under the sparkling stars in a blue-black sky.

Lucia pulled into a turnaround area and stopped the car. She rested her head on the steering wheel. "It won't be long, now. I'm doing fine. But thank the Lord Everett can take the wheel for the two hours to Mississippi." Their aged cousins, sisters, both in their late eighties, were putting them up. "What a treat! What a treat!" Cousin May had chirped over the phone, "Having you children with us again." Then she caught herself. "Oh my dear, I'm forgetting myself. We are all in grief for dear little Ann. She was like a sister to me." And Lucia knew Cousin May was getting Ann mixed up with their mother Ann.

Lucia lifted her head. The last day of his life Chris had said to her, "You're a youthful handsome woman, Lucia. I love that thick white hair and those gorgeous legs."

"You're crazy," Lucia had said, pinching his bottom as he walked past her toward the stern. A few moments later he had a heart attack and without a word fell overboard. She went down after him with life preservers, but he was dead, his white hair washing back and forth like anemones between his fishing line and the stern.

She put the Triumph in drive and moved out behind a state trooper. "Halleluja, I've got me an escort!" But the white car wove away at high speed and was lost to her. "Well. I'm on my own again." The rain had slowed to a drizzle when she turned toward the airport. The speeding cars and trucks in the six-lane interstate unnerved her, and she addressed her maker reverently each time she moved farther left, lane by lane. "Christ," she murmured when she spied the metal sign New Orleans International Airport that directed traffic to a new overpass she didn't know about. Her heart in her mouth, she managed to move back to the far-right lane. And the Triumph roared up the ramp and back over the traffic she had just left. Not daring to feel giddy, she found herself traveling parallel to jet runways. Strobelights marked the airport drive.

"That keeps those huge things from thinking this is another runway." Then she saw the sign telling her how to get short-term parking directions, and she was able to park on the first level. "I made it on instruments," she gasped, as she took the keys from the car. She was extremely stiff and in pain when she stood beside her car. "I'm too old for this." Two teen-aged boys looked backward at the old car, its classic body glittering in a coat of raindrops under the endless rows of fluorescent tubes. They grinned but looked concerned as they saw her effort to straighten her back and walk toward the elevator.

"I've never been in here unescorted."

"I beg your pardon?" said a young woman.

"Nothing. Nothing. Just talking to myself. Do it all the time." She wanted to get to a rest room.

Inside she began walking and scanning the crowd, looking for her tall younger brother. She was surrounded by a shifting sea of people speaking Spanish, French, Indian, and no telling what else, all under the nasal drone of the PA speaker. Her eyes, tired, swept over young, old, babies, nuns, sailors, people in wheelchairs, obese men and women waddling to and from the concourses. One very fat gray-haired man was bearing down on her, looking into her eyes, smiling. The smile caught her eye. Only that—that crooked half-smile.

"Everett?"

"What's the matter, Lucia? Don't you know me?" He was carrying a dark blue suit bag.

"Everett! I didn't" She closed her mouth with effort. "Everett," she said again.

He leaned forward and laid his cheek against hers briefly. "I reckon I have put on a little weight since you saw me last."

"Yes. Yes. I'm glad to see you, Everett. It's good you could come."

"I hate to put you out. Hope you didn't have any trouble. Was the weather good? I've been in here so long, I don't know what it's doing outside."

"The weather?" Oh yes, well, it rained a little. Nothing uh . . . let's go in here and order a cup of coffee or a Coke, maybe. I need to find a rest room. Are you hungry?"

"No. I just had a couple of hamburgers and a malt. I'm ready to roll. Ready to hit that interstate. Get on up to Cousin May and them's for some shuteye. I've been here over three hours."

"Well, I need something." And Lucia steered them into a coffeeshop. She went ahead and ordered coffee and a ham sandwich before going to a rest room.

"Oh, I guess I'll have one, too," said Everett. "And an order of fries. Traveling makes me hungry." Bulk made sitting difficult for him. "Have to fly first class. More room to spread out, you know."

"Excuse me, Everett," she murmured. "I'll be right back." She got up painfully.

"Why you're all crippled up!" He seemed surprised.

Lucia pressed her lips together and walked to the rest room. Inside a booth she sat down and began to laugh and cry. "This is hysterics. What am I going to do? I'm too tired to drive on. My God, he won't fit into the car."

"Is anything wrong?" came a voice from the next booth. "Do you need help?"

"No. Oh, no. Thank you. I just talk to myself. Sometimes what I say is funny, so I laugh . . ."

Silence.

The floodgates of Lucia's bladder opened, and for a moment she reveled in the greatest relief she had felt in days. She didn't say anything more aloud, but as she went out she patted her white bangs at the mirror and took a quick and satisfying look at her figure.

Everett was waiting for her. "I hate to see you so crippled up."

"Everett, what do you weigh, honey?"

"Three-twenty-five, right now." Then he gave one of his famous ha-ha-has. "Haven't you ever seen a fat man, Lucia?"

"It's just that I've never seen a 325-pound man in this family. You know, we all have tended to be slim. Slender." She wished she hadn't asked his weight.

"Well, you've seen one now," he said, steadying himself with the chair beside him. "These sure are little bitty old chairs."

Lucia laughed. They ate their sandwiches. "We may have a problem, Everett," she said, blotting the corners of her mouth with the stiff paper napkin.

"What's that?"

"Well, I drive a very small car. I'm just not perfectly sure you can get comfortable, completely comfortable . . . I was counting on you to drive us home . . ." She wanted to cry.

"You haven't gone and bought one of those little bitty old Jap cars have you?"

"No. No. Actually it's English. Belonged to my husband . . . it's small . . ." Her voice trailed off.

"Oh-oh." Everett's voice boomed, "I drive a Cadillac. Have to have a heavy car. Just kills my legs and back to ride in one of . . ."

"I really was counting on your driving. I'm not crazy about driving at night."

"Looks like you made it over here all right."

"Yes. Well, it wasn't easy."

"If I'd felt like driving, I'd have driven myself down in my Cadillac. We'll do okay. You got a pillow in it so I can stretch out?"

Chris's voice loomed in her ear. "Lucia, honey, you're being a fool. Tell that sonofabitch to get a taxi to a hotel."

Everett's face blanched when he saw the apple-green Triumph. "Lucia! Why in hell is an old lady like you driving this thing?"

Lucia was indignant. "Look, Everett, try to squeeze in. If you can't get in, we'll have to get you a room across the

Airline at the Hilton. This happens to be the only car I have."

He put his bag in the small trunk, muttering, "Ruining my good clothes," and stuffed himself into the little bucket seat. "Goddamn, Lucia. You'll have to bury me too when we get home. I still say 'home' even though the house is gone. And everybody is gone. Everybody but us. I can't believe Ann is gone. I kept thinking I'd come down to see her. We were close. A long time ago. Did she suffer much?"

"She suffered plenty. But she died peacefully."

"I'm glad to hear she went out easy." Then Everett began to wheeze. "I've got it too. We got it from Daddy. I quit smoking two years ago. Don't drink a drop," he added.

Lucia turned toward Baton Rouge.

"Here now. We're not going to Baton Rouge, are we?"

"Of course not. We turn north on I-55." Lucia hurt all over. She was getting a headache, and her eyes were too tired to cry. "Lord give me strength. What a fool I am."

"How's that?" Everett shouted over the engine.

She shook her head.

Everett tried to shift his bulk, but it was like trying to move a grapefruit in a demitasse spoon. "My circulation is going. In my legs," he hollered. He didn't have to shout.

"Mercy, Everett. Let me get out of this heavy traffic, and I'll stop every little while and let you get out and walk a bit."

But he grunted negatively, and she knew it was because it wasn't worth it to him trying to get out and back in. She turned north off the spillway interstate and drove in silence all the way to Lake Maurepas. "Let's stop at Heidenreidt's and get another cup of coffee. You can walk around."

"Okay, Lucia."

She parked the car near the door of the seafood restaurant which had been there as long as she could remember. "Make you nostalgic?"

"Yeah," said Everett, managing to extricate himself from the passenger seat. Lucia felt a terrible sadness over this baby brother she had once carried about like a ragdoll, who came home tall and thin and hurt from the long battle for the hills of South Korea and began his own battles in civilian life. A succession of jobs, two failed marriages, the loss of a young child. Poor boy.

In the old restaurant on the shore of Maurepas, Everett sat on a stool and ordered a dozen raw oysters. "Don't you want some, Lucia? My treat."

"No thank you, Everett."

"Remember how Daddy used to stop here on his way home from New Orleans and pick up a gallon of oysters? He and Mama would get in the kitchen and meal 'em up and season 'em and fry 'em in that big black iron skillet? Drain 'em on brown paper? Remember that big old white platter of Mama's? Heaped up, hot and crisp. Whooee!" He began dipping crackers in catsup and horseradish while an old black man shucked the oysters. "Y'all got any boiled crawfish?" he asked the sleepy waitress.

"Yeah. Want some?"

"Everett," said Lucia, "I'm afraid you'll be sick. And we need to be on our way pretty soon."

"Okay. Lord Jesus, I hate to think of stuffing myself back into that little bitty old car. How come you're driving that thing, hon? Now tell me the truth. You having a hard time, Lucia?"

"I've got some problems, Everett, but they don't have anything to do with my car or money. It was my husband's car, and I chose to keep it. Ordinarily, I just use a car to go to the post office and the A&P."

"Well, you made a mistake. You ought to get yourself a good heavy sedan."

"I'm sorry you're uncomfortable."

"I'm not complaining. I just hate to see you in such reduced circumstances."

"My circumstances are not reduced."

Everett dispatched a baker's dozen large raw oysters, lifting each, dipped red in the catsup mixture, to his mouth, and uttering a sound of appreciation of the taste.

They drove a long time on I-55 without talking. As they passed the Tangipahoa exit he said, "Was Ann right with her maker?"

"I beg your pardon?"

"Was she saved? Was she born again?"

"What in the hell are you talking about, Everett?"

"Don't blaspheme. She never was religious, Lucia. I wasn't either. Way back there. I'm just asking if you think my sister got right with the Lord."

Lucia was livid. "Yes," she said calmly, "I'm sure she and the Lord were on good terms."

"Well, I'm glad to hear it. After my last divorce I turned myself over completely to Jesus Christ, and I faithfully support Him."

"What church are you a member of? I know your last wife was Catholic."

"Don't belong to any. That is churchhouse. I support the Lord's work through several television ministries. They're saving souls like all getout all over the world. Did you ever think about how many souls are in hell, went there before the television came along and took the gospel to the farthest corner of the planet? Some people are going to rot in hell for persecuting these dedicated servants of the Lord who pack food to all those starving little boogers in Africa and all."

Lucia took her eyes off the highway for a split second to look at her brother. "You wouldn't possibly be including Louisiana's own, would you?"

"Most particularly. The Lord has simply put that poor fellow through a baptism of fire with Satan. The man's coming back. Just listen to him on the TV."

"I ran across him one time looking for a Saints game." They crossed the state line. "You're back in Mississippi, Everett."

Lucia tried to help her backache by pressing harder against the back of her seat. Since they had turned onto I-55 they had both been aware consciously or unconsciously that they were back in the world they knew best, the marshland above New Orleans, that edge of Louisiana that slid toward the state line, into the slow gentle sweep of low hills that meant Mississippi. Oh, it was different. A few miles made all the difference in the world.

"Yeah," he said. "I do appreciate your holding Ann's body till I could get here for the funeral."

"Body? I don't think you understand, Everett."

"Don't understand what?"

"This is to be a memorial service at the church. Ann's remains were cremated."

"Cremated! Cremated! Who is responsible for that?"

Rain was falling again. Lucia turned on the wipers. "It was Ann's wish."

"So! She wasn't saved! Of all the unholy, pagan things to do to my sister. You mean she's already . . . already burnt up?"

"Her remains are ashes."

"Well, I'll be goddamned."

"Now, who's blaspheming?"

"Why have I gone to all this trouble and expense and discomfort coming all the way down here from West Virginia? Huh? Tell me that?"

There just wasn't room in the little car for him to blow up. "I assumed you wanted to attend your twin sister's memorial service. We'll have an interment of the ashes in the plot. What's the difference?"

"Difference! I thought I was going to get to see her. See how she looked."

"I'm sorry you feel . . . cheated." Lucia's head was splitting. Her eyes were cloudy, and she cursed herself for where she was and wept inside for her baby sister and for Everett, who in no way resembled the boy or the man she remembered. She still had miles to travel. It must be nearly two o'clock. "What's a seventy-five-year-old fool doing on a highway this time of night? Morning."

"How's that?"

"Nothing, Everett. Just talking to myself."

"How long you been doing that?"

"Doing what?"

"Talking to yourself."

"A good while now. It was a deliberate decision. To talk to myself, I mean."

"For crying out loud. Are you bonkers?"

When Lucia saw Aunt May's porch light she moaned softly with relief.

"Listen, Lucia. I appreciate what you did—driving to New Orleans to get me. But I'll get a ride to Jackson and get a plane out of there to Charleston. Tomorrow afternoon, I guess. Late. Whenever this is all over—whatever it is we're having. Whatever you're having. Hell, I don't care. I mean . . ."

Lucia opened her door. The dome light cast a weak glow in the small space of the car. Her fingers held the cool metal of the handle as she searched Everett's profile, softened by age and shadow. Her only family, now. And she his. She smiled and laid her hand on his arm. "I understand. I know you'll be more comfortable in a big car. Wish I'd had a Cadillac just for tonight. Because I love you, Everett. I mean that."

"I know."

They walked through the fragrant, dewy grass toward Aunt May's porch.

In Aunt May's guest room, Lucia lay in the big four-poster she had first slept in and fallen out of before she could walk. Now, three quarters of a century later she did her deep-breathing exercise to relax. Deep, deep till her lower ribs bowed upward. The old house was quiet in the predawn darkness. Listening, remembering, as old houses do. Lucia let out a long breath. Such profound silence seemed to hold out a mystical beckoning. It wasn't the first time she had quite calmly thought she might die in her sleep. She inhaled.

The night after Chris died she had gone to bed in a friend's guest room, believing the enormous weight of sorrow would stop her heart as she slept. She had carefully arranged her arms on the covers so she would not be in disarray when they found her in the morning. But she had waked up in daylight, grateful to be alive and able to meet the day.

She exhaled and whispered to the dark room, "No. Twenty-four hours from now I'll be sound asleep in my own bed." The mattress pressed up against her as her body grew heavier, ever heavier, then moved weightlessly into the warm engulfing arms of sleep.

Elinor and Peggy

ELINOR HAD JUST driven into the shadowy car space between the pilings that supported the river house when the young woman ran up to her. Two days earlier, Elinor, still craving the aloneness she had found at the island, would have handily gotten rid of her. But last night she had admitted to herself, after being alone for two whole weeks, that she would like to have some company. So she smiled at the girl. And at herself for her change of mind. A breeze blew in from the river.

"I have to tell someone. I just saw a woman out in her front yard, naked," the girl blurted.

"What?" This must be the owner of the big station wagon and the two tow-headed kids Elinor had noticed from her kitchen window. Where on this highly secured island was anyone standing naked in her front yard? The front yard was the Kiawah River.

"Surely . . . ?"

"I'm sorry. My name is Peggy Gage. I'm staying in the house down there around the curve. I've been into Charleston, and coming back I took the shortcut to the island highway, and I saw something that makes me wonder if I'm hallucinating. I passed this house, and this woman got out of her car, pulling her clothes off, and by the time she got to her porch she was stark naked. I know this sounds crazy, but I just had to tell someone." Her chest rose with her quick gasp for breath.

"Good heavens," said Elinor, which was what she always said when she could think of nothing else to say. "Would you like to come in?" She shut her car door. "I stopped by the pier to add bait to my crabtrap." She looked at her fishy hands. "Come in and tell me about it. I need to wash my hands." Am I this lonely? she thought.

"Oh, I don't know . . ." The girl looked around nervously, as if unsure whether to continue her intrusion and tell her tale or to apologize and back away. She looked like a high school girl standing there in her tee shirt, shorts, and jogging shoes.

"Come on. I'll give you a cup of coffee and you can tell me about the naked lady."

They walked up the cypress steps to the deck and into the house. Reflections of the river flickered on the ceiling of the long living-dining room. The blend of shelter and tidal river never failed to move Elinor. It had something to do with the illusiveness of security. She poured coffee in the kitchen and carried the mugs to the big screened porch facing the river, now only a few yards out from the house, no sign of the sand and shell dunes that would appear in the late afternoon. She looked at the girl. "Now what was she doing?"

"Well, I had just dropped the boys off at Saint Michael's, and I took the shortcut heading back, and . . ." She set her mug on the glass-topped table between them and shook her head of dark close-cropped hair. "I pulled up at this corner for a red light, and all of a sudden I looked over at this little house and this big woman jumped out of her car, pulling her clothes off. She had her shirt off by the time she got out. She whipped off her big bra. You should have seen her. I couldn't believe my eyes. She was at least six feet tall, taller, maybe. I'm telling you! By the time she reached her porch she had on nothing but a pair of high-heeled pumps. Black patent spikes. The sun was so bright it sparkled on the black patent, and the pink skin was shiny. It was like she was illuminated, shining there for all the world to see."

"Good heavens," said Elinor. "What did she look like? Blonde? Brunette? Both?" She was startled to hear herself giggle.

"Blonde! Head full of bleached yellow kinks. Her body was so pink. A big woman. Get this: A really big woman, high-waisted, great big boobs kind of keg-shaped. Her hips were narrow—no bottom, like a man's. At her front door she yanked off her underpants. You see, she stomped in her high heels from the sidewalk to the front door, pulling things off as she went."

"Good heavens."

"She stood there a second, clutching her clothes. Then she threw them down like she was angry. She threw them, piece by piece, and her face looked angry, kind of desperate."

"How old did she look to be? Oh! Look at the dolphins. Usually they play on the other side of the river. Look how close!" The creatures leaped, arched out of the shimmering river.

"In her forties, maybe fifty. She was in good shape, though. Big but firm. Like a man, meaty. Actually she wasn't a blonde. That was plain to see. God, was she wild! And naked as a jaybird. Right out before the whole world. How can people do that? I didn't get your name."

"Elinor. Would you like some more coffee?"

"I guess not. Thank you. I'd better go. I'm working on my thesis. That's why we're living out here this fall. Ram goes into Charleston at 5:30. He's a surgeon." There was no hint of pride in her voice. "I run the boys in to Saint Michael's and usually get back before ten, to work. I'm supposed to get in three hours a day before I pick them up at three. It's Ram and Mother's idea." So Ram must be the young man in the white Peugeot.

Elinor walked to the door with Peggy Gage. "Well, what happened?"

"I just dropped out of the program for a while, had to when I got pregnant again . . ."

"No, I mean with the naked lady."

"Oh! The light turned green and I had to drive on. Just as I pulled away, the police car came, blue lights whirling and two policemen in it. They switched in front of me—I had to put on my brakes. She was so strange. Angry. And so pink. I just can't figure it out. Who called the police, I wonder . . ." Peggy Gage was a slender girl, her figure almost boyish. Her jogging shoes thumped softly on the plank stairs as she left.

Elinor latched the louvered screen. She was opening the dishwasher when the phone startled her.

"Hello." It was Louis. "It's been two weeks like I promised. How are you?"

"Doing all right. I've been down baiting my traps."

Louis laughed. I'm betting on you. I want to fly down Friday afternoon. Do you want to see me?"

"Of course . . . but . . ."

"But what? What are you afraid of?"

"You know what I'm afraid of, what this month down here is for. You must understand, Louis. I just can't get too deeply involved with anyone yet. Maybe ever."

"But we are deeply involved. I am. You are, too. I miss you terribly, Elinor. Let me come down for the weekend. I want to be with you, see this island you're so crazy about. Is it a pretty day down there?"

She looked out at a pileated woodpecker drilling away on a pine. "Oh, Louis, it's lovely. Lovely. I can hear the surf down on the beach. The river . . ."

"How about it?"

"All right. Shall I meet your plane?"

"I'll rent a car, Darling. I can't wait." Elinor could imagine his face, lines deepening around his blue eyes. Warm. Eager. Oh God. She hung up.

She put the coffee mugs into the dishwasher and shoved it closed. At the sink she turned on the water full-force and hosed out both sinks, slowly circling round and round, washing out every particle until the hot water made each stainless steel basin steam with heat. She cranked the casement open wide and felt the river breeze wash through the house from the porch doors through the window into the needle spray of pine boughs that brushed the screen.

On Wednesday morning there was a knock, and Elinor opened the door. "Peggy. Come in. Have you seen any more naked ladies?" She pushed the door open wider, hoping she had not sounded too flip with this tense-faced girl.

"No ma'am."

"I'll bring some coffee to the porch." Ma'am! Charleston.

When Elinor brought the steaming mugs, she found Peggy Gage settled comfortably on the chaise. "No, I drove back by there, though. Yesterday and this morning. There was no sign of her. I guess she was inside, or anyway somewhere with her clothes on. Maybe she's in jail."

"I doubt it," said Elinor, sitting down at the glass-topped table. "In a hospital, maybe, for observation." This could have been a pun, of sorts, but Peggy Gage didn't notice.

"Now, you see! You agree with me. There's something wrong with people who like to go around in front of other people naked. Just parading around with their . . . well, bare."

"I'm no authority on nudity or any other aberrant behavior."

"Do you know anyone who runs around in front of people naked?"

"Offhand, I can't think of anyone."

"Well, I'll tell you it's done. I can tell you one person who does it. Actually three." She took a sip of the coffee and recoiled from the heat.

"You know others?" Elinor turned her head to look squarely at the girl. What was this all about?

"Yes. My husband. And thanks to him, my two little boys don't like to wear clothes anymore. As soon as I get them home from school, they start pulling their clothes off. I have to say, 'Whoa!' "

Elinor looked back toward the river. High tide. She intended to walk down to the beach before lunch, not more than a quarter of a mile through the paths that ran along the river, and there it was, the Atlantic Ocean pushing its white ruffle of surf out of the blue deep, over the creamy sand. On and on. Over and over. Ever and ever. A reminder that nature's arrangements can go on forever.

Penny Gage set the mug on the table beside the chaise and casually pulled her jeans away from her crotch. "Ram thinks people ought to go naked at home. He does it all the time, and he encourages the boys to do it. In Charleston they swim naked; well, that's not anything, of course, but he lets them run around in the front yard without a stitch on. And in front of guests at night. I just don't think it's normal."

"Can you control that sort of thing? I mean, make rules about when and where . . . draw the line, so to speak?"

"Oh, you don't know Ram. I've tried, but he makes fun of me. Tells the boys, 'Listen to Mom, guys. She's so modest. Ashamed of her bod!'" Peggy Gage mocked her husband's voice angrily. Whatever the girl's state of mind, this Ram must be a pain. "I don't want to make a huge issue of it, but I'm sick of it. It's come to symbolize Ram's whole personality."

"How old are they?"

"The boys are three and four. Ram is thirty-two."

"Well, Ram doesn't go into the front yard nude, does he?"

"Oh, no, of course not. He even wears his briefs in the pool, except at night sometimes. Even I skinnydip at night. I'm not a prude. But he walks all over the house naked, strolls through the family room, sits in his study, comes through the kitchen, opens the fridge. And drinks a gulp of tea—right out of the pitcher. In front of me and the boys, and he thinks I'm all up-tight because I won't do it. Just wants our own little household nudist colony. I think he's disgusting. What do you think?"

"Well, I don't know Ram. And I've never had reason to give much thought to the subject of nudity in the home. I have no children . . ."

"Are you married?"

"I was." Elinor expected to be asked if she was a widow or divorced, but Peggy held to her subject.

"Did your husband roam through the house with his thing bouncing around in front of him like something on a leash? Pretending to be perfectly natural? Acting like . . ."

Elinor looked at a great blue heron flapping heavily over the river, almost in the water. "No, he didn't." No, he certainly didn't.

Peggy stood up. "I think there's something wrong with Dr. Ramsey Gage. I think he likes to see his sons running around like that because he sees some kind of extension of his own masculinity in them. He's insecure! It's some kind of nutty reassurance he needs. It's ruined my sex life with him, I can tell you."

Elinor stood up, too, and moved quickly through the living room to the front door. She said, "Did you see the flounder fishermen out in the boats last night with the lights? I saw two men bring in at least ten big ones down at the pier, yesterday."

"Yes, I saw them. They catch them night and day out there." Peggy started down the stairs. At the landing she stopped and pulled a leaf off a bay branch and said, "I hope you don't think I'm awful. It's just that I'm kind of tired of living out here by myself all day, not having an adult to talk to . . ."

"No, indeed I don't," said Elinor, with a reassuring wave of her hand. "Goodbye." She latched the door and leaned on it a moment. This was shampoo and manicure day, and she could get that in before her walk. She went into her bathroom and stripped off her clothes, tossing everything into the wicker hamper. In the shower she shielded her nipples from the needle stings of the water. Stepping out she threw her dripping hair back off her face and stood looking at her wet self in the mirrored wall behind the dressing table.

Suddenly she laughed and grabbed a big yellow towel and made a sarong for herself. In the bedroom she pulled the spread back and lay down where she had a full view of the river, not two hundred feet away. She thought of her former husband, Arnold, whom she had not seen for two years. No troublesome image arose; he was at last becoming a past event, not so much a person whose memory pained her to distraction. She had found the strains of separation and divorce almost unbearably hard.

She thought of Louis, who had quickly sensed that he must not come on strong, who listened intently, carefully, when she said she could not possibly allow anybody in her life for a long time, for as long as it took for confidence to come back, for things to unravel, completely if possible. She had known him for nearly a year now. He had shown more than casual interest in her the evening they met at a party. He had guided her to an empty sofa and brought a drink for her. His wife had died, he told her, and he asked why she had divorced Arnold, who was a successful doctor.

Sipping on her drink, she heard herself telling a stranger, "I was used. Blatantly. In every way. Psychologically, physically, financially, you name it. I was also patronized. I was absurdly slow to realize all this and slow to act when I did see it. It took me two years to get out of my confusion and see a lawyer. Arnold did not contest. He was already involved with someone else—had been with several, I was told."

"Will you marry again?"

"Probably not."

Louis' manner and rugged good looks had made him a comfortable companion. He never questioned her about Arnold again. But he obviously wanted her. "I have to have time, Louis," was all she said. But over the months she'd grown fond of him. If she could love, she loved him. Still, she remained wary. She sometimes thought of herself as a cat, treed, sitting on a limb near the trunk, watchful, afraid to come down, afraid of being stroked. Ready to spring away.

Now, the image of Louis did stand before her as if framed in the wide window, the river glittering like a ribbon, moving back toward the ocean, behind him. She wanted to see him . . . Her pillow was getting damp. She sighed and rolled over, pulling the towel from around her body and making a bright yellow turban for her head.

On Friday afternoon Elinor drove down to the floating pier, which rose and fell with the tide. She could have walked on the trail through the woods, but she hoped to harvest more crabs today from her trap than she could carry back on foot. A big box lined with newspaper was on the back seat.

She was on her knees struggling to pull the wood-framed trap to the surface when Peggy Gage came smacking her rubber soles down the ramp to the pier. She rapped her knuckles on the fish-cleaning sink to announce herself.

"Do you have a good catch?"

"I can't tell yet. The bloody trap is really too heavy for me." Elinor let the rope go, thinking she could do better if she rested a while. The trap splashed and sank heavily, sucking surface water down with it.

"Let me try," said Peggy, and she began to slowly hoist the wet rope, hand over hand. "It is heavy," she said, but she brought it to the surface. It hit the underside of the pier roughly. "Gosh, look at the crabs!"

Together they dragged the big crate over the edge of the flooring and set it on the pier. As the water drained away, the frenzied crabs clicked and bubbled, and the two women bent over them, counting silently. "I count seventeen," said Elinor. "How many do you see?"

"I count eighteen, but they move so fast it's hard to be sure. These are real beauties, not a throwback in here." And they were, with flailing bright blue claws grasping at the chicken-wire sides and at each other, the claws, the greenish spiky shells large and obviously heavy with meat. Peggy expertly bounced the trap over on its side, throwing the glistening, struggling crabs into a wet, writhing heap. "When they start trying to crawl out the opening, we'll catch them with the clamps and drop them into your box."

"Let's rest a minute," laughed Elinor, thankful that she had an expert on hand for her big catch. "I'm exhausted. I'm older than you are."

"You don't look old."

"Well, I feel it right now," said Elinor. She expected Peggy to say how old? but she didn't. She was prepared to tell her, honestly, forty-seven.

They sat flatly on the weathered boards of the pier, leaning back on their hands, their legs out in front of them. Elinor looked up at the blue sky and waited to hear about nudity.

"Well," said Peggy, as if she had heard her cue. "Ram and I had it out last night. He came wagging into the kitchen to fix his drink . . ."

"Nude?"

"As a jaybird. I turned around and just looked at him like this."

Elinor looked respectfully as Peggy sat forward and put her hands on her hips and stared at her with lowered lids. There was a new confidence in her voice. The plaintive tone almost gone. "I told him I had had it, to go put some clothes on or else. And to put the boys' pajamas on them when they got out of the tub. Not to bring them in here with their little tally-whackers bouncing and him saying, 'Look, Mom! Look at these guys.' I said, 'Do that one more time and I'm getting Tag Benjamin onto you.'"

"Who is Tag Benjamin?"

"A psychiatrist, that's who. He looked after Nini Johnston when Joe had an affair with his nurse, and you wouldn't believe how he toughened her up. Listen, I had to take a stand."

"Was psychiatric counseling your final stand?"

"No, divorce would have been my final stand. But listen, it

worked. Surgeons are such little prima donnas. They're afraid
of the psychiatric solutions." She laughed a new, deep infec-
tious laugh that Elinor was glad to hear. It seemed to say, I'm
okay.

"It's a pity that you had to threaten him," Elinor said, slapping a gnat on her upper arm. "God, I hope these gnats aren't
going to swarm like they did after the big rain last week."

"What really got to him, I think, was I just told him flat out
what this has been doing to me. I never had any brothers. My
father was the soul of modesty. I've never seen my mother
without her clothes on. We're just funny people, I guess, for
the times. Ram knows all this. So to me there is—or used to
be—a mystery about men, a kind of romance about their
bodies. Crazy or not, I like that. So here I was the only female
in the house, not about to traipse around naked. And all I
could see in every direction was penises, all sizes, all states.
They had gotten common. I was sick of the sight of them.
There was no mystery. None. I couldn't stand the thought
of . . ."

"Yes," said Elinor, with some finality.

"Do you get the picture?"

"Yes, clearly." Elinor looked at her dirty hands, glad she had
waited to do her nails.

"I mean penises, penises, penises."

"I know."

"You do?"

"Well, I mean I do get the picture."

Peggy lay on her back and laughed, the sound carrying
across the river and the marshes, and with it the last tinge of
anguish. "This is the life, isn't it? Charleston's gotten to be
pretty much like other cities now, but out here you get those
feelings of 'low country' that people talk and write about. It's
different."

"It really is."

The crabs had settled down. Their protest seemed exhausted, too. The great blue claws seemed frozen to the wire of the trap and to each other. Still. "I don't want them to die before I can get them to a pot of boiling water," said Elinor.

"Don't worry. They'll live for hours," said Peggy. "So I screamed all this at him, and you know what?"

Elinor looked at the girl, who sat up and grasped the long clamps with which every river house was equipped along with a huge kettle.

"I'll tell you what. He went back and put on those maroon and white windowpane-checked pajamas Mother gave all three of them to match for Christmas, and they came back to the kitchen sweet as you please. Covered!"

"What did he say? Anything?"

"He said, 'Okay, okay, OKAY!'" Peggy's voice got louder with each okay. "And I'm tempted to believe he meant it. For once I think he took the time to think about what I was saying to him."

"Well, that certainly sounds like progress. What do you think the naked woman in Charleston had to do with it all? Anything?"

"I don't know just what. For sure she did get me to thinking harder about it. I mean my situation with Ram. I wonder what happened to that great big pink angry woman."

"Did you tell Ram about her?"

"I sure did. I told him the police were picking her up. I also told him I had an idea her husband had a nudity mania, and she likely just lost her mind and tore off her clothes out in the street."

"What did he say to that?"

"At first he laughed and said I was probably making it all up. Then he said he wished he'd been there. Actually, he wasn't interested. He looks at naked people all day long." A large crab began to crawl through the opening along the edge of the trap, and Peggy deftly clamped it across the back of its broad shell. The crab fought angrily with his claws, but they were useless in her grip. She dropped the crab into the box and picked up another one. "Do you like she-crab soup?"

"I had some in Charleston that was delicious."

"Do you know how to tell the difference between a he-crab and a she-crab?"

"Is that a joke?"

"No! Look." And she turned the crab over showing the white undershell. "This is called the apron, and this long thing that you catch hold of to get the shell off means it's a male. The female just has a little roundish one without the handle."

Elinor looked at Peggy helplessly. "I'm still a novice."

"It's against the law to take a she-crab, and we used to grate egg yolks instead of the crab roe in the soup. It's almost as good." She dropped the he-crab into the box.

"Where are your little boys today? Is your husband home early?"

"He'll be in any time, now. The boys are staying in Charleston with Mother for the weekend." She tossed a she-crab into the river.

"That's nice."

"It is nice. And safe. She has everything for them, a whole play-yard. All safe. And Sunday she'll dress them up and take them to Sunday school and to the club for buffet." She dropped another crab into the river, then the last crab into the box. "But of course I know what she's really up to."

"What's that?" said Elinor, knowing the answer.

"She wants another grandchild. She hopes that if we're out here honeymooning it up alone on weekends, I'll get pregnant."

"What about your thesis? You said she wants you to get your master's."

"Oh, she's counting on me to come through with all of it. What are you going to do with all these crabs? Are you expecting guests for the weekend?"

"Yes, I am," said Elinor.

"Well, that's different. I hope they like crabs. You have enough for quite a party. How many?"

"Only one."

"Man?"

"Yes."

"Can he boil crabs?"

"I'm not absolutely sure about him, but I'm pretty good at it."

"Sounds like a nice evening. If you have some crabmeat left over, and you certainly will, you can make crab omelet for breakfast. Do you know how to make that?"

"You're too kind, Peggy. I really do appreciate your handling the crabs for me. But the gnats are picking up, and I want to get these into the sink."

"Yes, I have to go in, too. We're going to the Pirate's Cove over at the marina for dinner." She carried the box of crabs up the ramp, her back arched, and set them in Elinor's car. "Maybe I'll see you next week," she said, and with a wave of her hand she ran on toward her house.

Elinor turned water on the crabs in the sink, stirring them to a renewed flurry of helpless clawing and rattling. She set the enormous pot out on the counter and put a box of crab seasoning beside it. She looked at the clock on the range and hurried from the kitchen. It was later than she thought.

After showering, she put on a white cotton blouse and a long skirt with lush roses splashed over it. She looked closely at her brown hair as she brushed it off her forehead, fluffing it dry till it shone. She walked barefoot to the porch chaise in time to watch the pink and blue and lavender sunset over the marsh, streaking and blending like watercolor on wet paper.

Slowly the white egrets dropped down, silhouettes against the merging tints of the sky, collecting on the long sand spit rising from the river, pecking over the goodies among the rocks and shells in the glistening surface. The afternoon kingfisher emitted its rattling cry and plunged into the water. It darted up, a small fish in its beak, as the great blue heron made a slow-motion landing among the egrets.

"Incredible," said Elinor softly, as she did every afternoon. "Incredible."

Listening, she heard Ram Gage's little sports car roar up the road, and she sat there waiting for Louis.

Miss Robbie's Cup of Tea

MISS ROBBIE felt more than a little foolish taking the silver teapot out of the china cabinet, but she meant to serve tea to her husband, Albert. Tea had been in the back of her mind for a week or two, thoughts of calling three or four friends, women she hardly ever saw anymore, saying, "Come over tomorrow afternoon for a cup of tea." Like that. Casual. A quiet civilized little ritual she would like to get into. She had a teapot and cups and more than one sugar and cream set, sugar spoon, her mother's Madeira tea napkins—some tissue-thin but ironed smooth as silk with their little blue-gray edges and cutwork corners. She had everything she could possibly need to serve tea graciously, including a nice parlor to serve it in. So why didn't she do it? She wished she knew. Everything was habit. If it was possible that she could form such a habit, she would start it with Albert.

Suddenly this afternoon she decided she would just serve tea to Albert and herself. She didn't ask him if he cared for tea. She knew he didn't. Albert liked beer. His whole corner of the den smelled of it; his chair, the pillow, everything. His bedroom. He moved in its aura. She wondered—if Albert ever left for any reason—whether she could get the smell out. How would she go about it? Air fresheners? Never. They were worse than beer. Open windows? Hardly. Louisiana air wilted the lampshades and draperies if you opened the windows.

You had to keep the place shut up and the air conditioning on no matter how pretty it was outside in the spring and the fall, and certainly in the summertime. Once in a while she had tried it when the weather seemed too perfect to shut out, but it didn't work. Albert's shoes got covered with mildew in his closet—the color of the embroidery on those Madeira tea napkins. She had taken all his shoes outside and wiped them inside and out with a damp cloth and let them dry in the hot sunshine.

She rubbed hard on the fat belly of the teapot till she could see herself reflected on the bulge, not clearly but a face with glasses and with gray hair like a halo. Closest to the teapot her nose looked strangely large.

She washed the pot out carefully so the tea would not taste like detergent. Then she dried it and hung two teabags over the edge and put the kettle on to boil water.

She heard Albert getting out of his chair. She heard his slippers scuffing on the den rug. He didn't pick his feet up by this time of day. Teatime.

"What are you doing?" Albert asked, looking at the pot.

She was ashamed of her temptation to say something like, "Oh, currying old Dobbin," or "panning for gold." Albert didn't deserve sarcasm. He was developing cataracts, and Miss Robbie dreaded the day when he would have to have the first one removed. Everyone said it didn't amount to a row of pins anymore to remove them with a laser; you could go home the same day. But the thought of Albert having it done made her sad and a little frightened.

"Oh, I just thought I'd polish the teapot," she said, holding it up to catch the afternoon sun shining through the mini-blinds in the kitchen window. "Pretty, isn't it?"

Albert grunted, not crossly. He never could understand why she always had to be doing something, always ginning around. "I thought when you retired from teaching you'd retire," he would say. Albert had retired as a CPA the same year she had, and he had indeed retired. Miss Robbie couldn't understand how he just trudged into the den every morning and turned on Jane Pauley and sank into his old chair while she got his breakfast—orange juice, grits with butter, and bacon. Every morning. She took secret pleasure in dripping the decaffeinated Community dark roast coffee, which he depended upon for his "pickup" with breakfast. He never knew the difference.

"Nothing but commercials," she heard him mutter, back in his chair. "Nothing but advertising in the paper. Money, money, money, money." He flicked the remote to Ted Turner's news station, where for the fifth or sixth time he would hear of the most unspeakable horrors from all over the world. Multiple murders; plane crashes; hearses pulling away from an execution site; and every living creature on God's green earth either mating or giving birth, in the wild, in captivity, and in the bed. Through it all, Albert just sat there drinking his beer.

Miss Robbie worked faster. She wanted to surprise him. She wanted to overwhelm him, in fact, appear with the elegantly appointed tray, so tempting, so labored over, he could not turn down her offer of tea.

She took the round tray out of silver cloth and set the pot on it. She added two teaspoons, a sugar spoon, the sugar bowl. She took a lemon out of the crisper and quickly cut two thin slices, which she laid on a small saucer, deftly stabbing each with a whole clove. From the dining room chest she lifted out two of the delicate napkins and laid them carefully near the pot, one cutwork corner showing its scallops under a corner of the other.

"I'll use his grandmother's teacups," she thought. He talked about his grandparents more and more lately, seeming to feel increased respect for them as he got older. Miss Robbie had only two of the cups. Small, thin old Haviland, with low embossing and pale pink rose garlands around their sides. There were no saucers, only the two cups, but Miss Robbie had wanted them when Albert's mother died. They were so pretty and delicate, rather lonely looking, left there on the back of a shelf saucerless. And Miss Robbie had often fancied the grandmother, whom she never knew but whose picture hung in their hall, ruching and cameo under her patrician chin, serving tea at the parsonage in Alabama where Albert's grandfather had preached for forty-six years.

She knew exactly what to do. She took two plain white porcelain demitasse saucers out of the kitchen cabinet and set them under the cups. Oh-oh! The cups were not clean. There was a large roach leg lying in one. She lathered them up under the hot tap, rinsed and dried them, careful not to drop one in her haste.

As a final touch she stepped out the back door and snapped off a daffodil and laid it on the tray. Oh, how lovely, she thought, lifting the boiling kettle. She filled the pot half full and carried the tray to the parlor and edged it onto the coffee table, pushing to one side a candlestick, a cachepot, a pen, and a magazine with Picasso on its cover. Ugly little man.

"Albert," she called, "come into the living room with me . . ." She sat down carefully on the sofa, smiling to herself, for she felt a little silly, acting like a young wife for no good reason on earth other than her own unexplained whimsy.

"Albert?"

"I'm coming. I'm coming." She heard his slippers hiss on the kitchen linoleum. "Just a minute. Just a minute." She heard the refrigerator door open and thump closed. Then a familiar swush-snap as Albert came into the living room, his freckled hand wrapped around a cold can of beer.

"Albert!"

"What!"

"Albert, I want to serve tea."

"To who?"

"To you and me! I want us to have tea."

"Tea?" He was honestly nonplussed.

"Well, why not? Look how lovely . . ."

Albert tilted his head back and drained out a long draft as if to ensure his commitment to his own choice of beverage. No turning back for tea. Miss Robbie clasped her hands tightly on her knees, her knuckles white as chicken bones. She felt terribly foolish now. Albert belched.

"Excuse me," he said politely. Oh, Albert had nice manners. He was a perfectly nice man. He came from lovely people. "Listen, I didn't know you were making tea for me. You know I don't drink hot tea, Robbie. Why'n't you call in some lady if you wanted to have tea." Obviously put upon, he tipped the can up again and walked through the dining room to the kitchen.

Miss Robbie sat there on the sofa before the tea things unsure whether to continue her tea. Absently she picked up the magazine and looked more closely at the image of Pablo Picasso's dark menacing face. "Ugly little man," she said softly, and without taking her eyes off his black ones took up the pen on the coffee table. She was not ready to throw away the *Atlantic,* but she was tired of that face.

With the bold black ink she drew a big grid of Teddy Roosevelt teeth across the grim mouth, as bold and bare as a skeleton's. She pulled his black eyes to the inside so that he was crosseyed. She gave him heavy eyebrows and hung bangs over his domed forehead. She tossed the magazine to one side. She hadn't changed Picasso at all. Then as she reached angrily for the teapot, the doorbell rang. The devil take Albert, she thought, as she walked to the foyer.

A small Girl Scout smiled up at her. "Would you like to buy some cookies?"

"Hello!" said Miss Robbie. The child's face was fresh and sunny. "Do you girls still sell Savannah?" she asked, smiling into the upturned face.

"No ma'am. You mean Samoas? I have them and some Do-Si-Dos." She began reaching into her shoulder bag.

"Oh. Well, just a moment while I get my purse," said Miss Robbie, hurrying to her desk in the den.

"Who's that?" said Albert.

Miss Robbie didn't answer him. She wondered what neighbor's child or grandchild the little girl could be. She went back to the door and while she waited for her change she said suddenly, "I have just made tea. Why don't you come in and have tea with me? It's hot and we can have Do-Si-Dos with it. Do you have time?"

The little girl peered into the foyer beyond Miss Robbie. Her eyes took on a wider look, almost afraid. "Oh, no ma'am. I can't." She dropped some coins into Miss Robbie's hand.

"Oh, come on. It'll be fun. I have some adorable little cups you'll just love." She stood to one side and gestured toward her living room.

"No'm, I can't. My mother told me not to go into any stranger's house. She told me that this very afternoon."

Miss Robbie laughed, fighting off offense. "But I'm no stranger. I've lived here for thirty years. I used to teach little girls like you. For years and years. They called me Miss Robbie. I can call your mother. What is her name?"

But the child held her cap to the back of her curly blonde head and hurried down the walk.

Miss Robbie shut the door and turned the deadbolt. She returned to the sofa. Picasso stared at her relentlessly through the inked doodles. Of course the child was right. What a smart, wise little girl she was. Through the living room window Miss Robbie watched the little legs walking rapidly toward the house next door, the shoulder bag lighter by two boxes.

Miss Robbie poured tea into one of Albert's grandmother's little teacups. She pinched a drop from a thin lemon slice over the tea, spooned a bit of sugar into it, and stirred. Hm-m-m. How good it was. She sat sipping the tea and smiling to herself a little bemused by what it all meant. She had had no reason to assume that Albert would accept a cup of tea, and the little scout was perfectly right not to come into a stranger's house. If forthrightness was virtue, she had experienced virtue this afternoon and should feel gratified. But I'm tired, she thought, of ending every frustration by counting my blessings. She reached for the magazine and tore off the face of Picasso. Slowly she tore the paper across his face, then down between his frown lines then across again and down again until all that was left was a handful of small bits of paper. She dropped them into the cachepot.

In the den Albert cleared his catarrh, sounding like a bull alligator down in the marsh, like he would surely choke to death. But Miss Robbie knew he would not, for he had been doing it this way for longer than she could remember. She stirred her tea, the spoon grating on a few grains of un-dissolved sugar.

She sighed and looked around the quiet room. "I'll just have another cup," she said softly, and lifted the polished teapot.

The Mercy of the Lord

THE FIRST NIGHT Aunt Mamie D. was with us she came to my door and asked me to sleep with her.

"What's the matter, Aunt Mamie D.?" I said, "Are you scared in our creaky old house?"

"No, I'm not scared, but I figured I'd go right to sleep after I said my prayers, but I didn't, and I thought we might talk a little and we'd both go to sleep."

I got up and followed her down the dimly lit hall. In her long dimity nightgown, she was short and shapeless and cushiony looking. She padded silently ahead of me in little felt slippers with fuzzy balls on the tops, and her white hair was held close to her head in a hairnet. Without her glasses, her eyes looked undressed, naked. She had ridden eighty miles on a bus to come and stay with us.

"What are you all doing in there?" It was Brother on the sleeping porch. "Be quiet in there. I'm trying to sleep." I was surprised he was awake. He was usually out the minute his head touched the pillow. Brother and I were twins.

Aunt Mamie D. and I went into Mama and Daddy's room where she was spending the nights while they were gone. She had already told me she could not sleep under the ceiling fan, and it was too damp on the sleeping porch, she said. So we just lay down there with the barest breeze coming through the bay window. I wondered how far Mama and Daddy had gotten on their trip to Chattanooga. Daddy said they might spend the night in Birmingham.

"Let's name trees," said Aunt Mamie D. in her quaky low voice.

"Ma'am?" Aunt Mamie D. was my great aunt, the sister of my grandmother, and she seemed like a link to a time long ago and to people I should have known but didn't.

"Don't you know how to name things alphabetically to put yourself to sleep?"

"No'm." I was sleepy and didn't need putting to sleep. "How do you play?"

"Let's name all the trees we can think of beginning with A: Ash, alder, aspen, apple . . . you name one, Sister." Her voice sounded thin to me, like soft wind blowing through reeds that dry up in late summer and become little pipes, all blended in that hissy way to say ash . . . aspen . . .

"You must know one," she said. "Name one."

"Well, you named all of them before I even got started."

"All right, then, B. Bay, blackthorn, black gum, balsa, blue spruce."

She'd done it again. "Banana," I blurted. "C! Chinaberry, chinquapin, chestnut, cow oak, cherry, coconut." Aunt Mamie D. didn't name any C's. I heard her begin to make bubbly noises with her mouth and nose at the same time. I raised up on my elbow and I could barely make out her face. Her mouth was open. I crept out of the bed and went back to my own room. The curtains bulged like the cheeks of the west wind, and when I lay down the deep-belly croak of our bullfrogs came in on the soft breeze. Overhead my two red-headed sisters were still up, moving around their room bare-foot, packing their clothes to leave tomorrow for the Holmeses' camp down at the mouth of the Tchefuncte River right at Lake Pontchartrain. I lay there and thought about Mama and Daddy staying in a fine hotel somewhere and Mama putting on a hat and gloves just to go down to the dining room to eat supper, like she did at the Edwards House in Jackson last summer when Brother and I went with them on the trip to see Daddy's tall sisters. I thought how lonely Aunt Mamie D. must be to have to play games alone at night to put herself to sleep because she had no husband to talk and whisper with after the lights were out.

Suddenly it was full daylight, and I heard Aunt Mamie D. rattling pots in the kitchen. And I heard Brother. "Aunt Mamie D., I don't know where that stuff came from, but I ain't going to eat oatmeal."

"It came from your mother's pantry, Brother, so she must expect you children to eat it."

I ran to the kitchen. "We feed it to the goldfish," I said. "And Oleander puts it in cookies, but we don't eat it all mushy in a bowl like this. But Brother, I'm going to count every time you say *ain't* and tell Mama." I noticed he had his hightop tennis shoes on.

"Son, you're too fair to go out in those overalls without a shirt. You'll have water blisters on that white skin."

"And any other bad language," I continued.

"No'm," Brother hooked his thumbs in the bib, ignoring me. "I'm going to be working on my treehouse with Otis, Jr., and it ain't nothing but shady up in all those mulberry leaves."

"Ain't, ain't," I said, but nobody noticed.

"I want chocolate and one piece of toast buttered on both sides," Brother demanded. "Where's Oleander?"

"She's getting her week off while your folks are in Tennessee," said Aunt Mamie D. "We don't need help. Your mother is dependent on darkies, but I'm not. I haven't had help since I left my papa's house." And she went about setting the breakfast before Brother.

We heard thumping above us. "What do those two eat?" asked Aunt Mamie D., spooning some white powder into a jelly glass and raising her eyes right quick to the ceiling like Brother Hawkins did when he mentioned heaven in a sermon. "We ought to all sit down together and start the day with a prayer and a good hot breakfast." She ran some water

over the powder and stirred it while it fizzed and sparkled
close to her face. And while it was making diamonds on her
fuzzy upper lip she drank the stuff down.

"What is that?" asked Brother, and he might as well have
held his nose and added *phew!*

"It's Sal Hepatica," said Aunt Mamie D. "I take a little
glassful every morning." She set the glass in the sink and
ran it over with water. Brother looked at me over the rim of
his cup.

"Are both of you children regular?"

Before I could tell her that Brother had to take Cascara lots
of times, Otis, Jr., Gordon split the air with his two-finger
whistle in the backyard. "Hey, Brother," he yelled, "Let's get
going." And Brother jumped up and tore out the back door. I
looked out and saw that Otis, Jr., had his hatchet, which he
claimed was as sharp as a razor.

"Brother," I screamed, "don't you touch Otis, Jr.'s hatchet!
You know what Mama said." I could just see him with a
big gash in his leg and all his blood gushing out before we
could put a tourniquet on him and save him. I could see
Mama coming home and finding him gone. And that box
Elise warned me about when I walked about the house barefoot on winter nights: *If you catch cold and die from cold
feet, you'll be put into a box and buried deep, deep under the
ground.* "Brother!"

Aunt Mamie D. hurried after him with her short steps, but
he and Otis, Jr., were already down in the back of the lot.
Daddy had told Brother he and Otis, Jr., could use lumber
from the pile behind the shed where our poor Jersey heifer had
lived, and he bought Brother a hammer and a big bag of nails.
"You're nearly nine years old, Son. It's time you had your own
hammer. Remember two things: Don't let me catch you with
my hammer again, and don't go out there barefooted."

Our parents had left many instructions with us and with
Aunt Mamie D., all things that we must not do. Brother must
not go out in the yard barefoot. The night before they left,

Daddy put his car keys in the library table drawer and said sternly to everyone, "Sarah, my car is not to leave this place. Do you understand?" He was just teaching Sarah to drive, and she begged him every day to let her go out alone. We all acknowledged his command seriously except for Sarah whose eyes widened with hurt that she should be singled out as a possible culprit in such an unthinkable act. There were other rules for Brother and me. We must not climb on the book-cases; we must not plug anything in that was electrical; we must not catch bees; we must not go swimming. All these were based on some past experience they had had with us.

After Brother and Otis, Jr., began their work and while Aunt Mamie D. spent considerable time in the bathroom, I went to my room to make up the bed and dress. She was going to let me help her make one of her jam cakes. Pretty soon she came in and raised her head so she could see me through her bifocals. "Well, this is nice," she said, patting the pillows and lining up my dolls on the cedar chest. She didn't go upstairs. Sarah and Elise had brought their suitcases and phonograph and boxes down and set them on the front porch even though it was hours till the Holmeses were picking them up. Aunt Mamie D. took a pitcher of water out there and watered all Mama's ferns and the big tuberous begonia on the stand by the door.

"Well, Sister," she said finally, "let's go make our jam cake."

"I can't wait," I said. "Are you going to let Brother and Otis, Jr., lick the bowl?"

"We'll see. Maybe I'll give them the bowl and you can have the icing pan."

She made a spice cake and raked a whole pint of blackberry jam into the batter. She beat it with a wooden spoon till I thought her arm would fall off and poured it into three layer pans that were all buttered and floured. After she put the pans into the oven she got out the double boiler to make boiled icing. While the Karo and sugar and water heated up she beat eggwhites till they were stiff, and when the sweet stuff was cooked she took it to the window to let it cool. Just as she set the pan on the sill, just at that very moment, Daddy's little black coupe whizzed past in reverse.

"For mercy's sake," gasped Aunt Mamie D., grabbing her throat. "What on earth?"

"They've taken Daddy's car out," yelled Brother, as he and Otis, Jr., headed through the house to the front porch. By the time Aunt Mamie D. had trotted up the hall, Brother and Otis, Jr., and I were standing on the banisters, clutching the posts, and screaming, "Look! Look! Look at them!"

Sarah had made a right turn through Mama's flags into the front yard, but now she was wrenching the steering wheel to the left. It was the most thrilling sight I'd ever witnessed.

"Girls! Girls!" quaked Aunt Mamie D.'s little voice. "Stop it! Stop it! Get out of that car this minute!" She wrung her hands. "Lord have mercy. Get out of there! Sa-rah!"

But Sarah had now mastered the sharp left and was circling Mama's big Cheerful japonica that had been taken up at her Papa's old home with a block and tackle. Beside her was Elise, shrieking and laughing and holding onto the door, while Sarah leaned way over against her door, her hands clamped to Daddy's steering wheel. She had on lipstick that made her teeth look white as chalk, and her big smile showed she had never had so much fun in all her life. They drove around in the circle at least ten times and never would have stopped, I guess, but a front tire hit the domino bricks along the driveway and the engine coughed and died. Our porch and our yard were silent for a few seconds, then Brother and Otis, Jr., began to yell like crazy, and I shouted, "Daddy said you couldn't do that. He's going to wear you out, Sarah. You, too, Elise. You're sitting right up there beside her."

"Daddy wouldn't do any such thing." That was Sarah. Somehow I believed her. She was far too brave and daring for anyone to punish her like a child.

Aunt Mamie D. had not bargained for all this. "Sarah," she said, "you put that thing back in the garage. You will just have to answer to Mr. Warner." That was one of her funny ways. She called Daddy Mr. Warner. She called Mama Ellen, but of course Mama was her own sister's child. She could hardly call her Mrs. Warner. Sarah cranked the car up without any trouble and drove back through the flag bed and down the driveway into the garage.

Aunt Mamie D. hurried out to the yard. "Let me try to set up these poor irises. Ellen dotes on her irises so. Brother, you and Sister come help me set these bricks back in a row. Mercy, mercy, mercy." Sarah and Elise helped. They thought they were so smart.

"Daddy laid down the law to you all," I said. "You know what he said."

"He said we couldn't take it away. And we didn't. We just drove around the front yard," and she and Elise laughed and threw back their long red hair.

"Both of you march straight upstairs and sit there until Mr. Holmes comes for you." Aunt Mamie D. pointed her finger toward the house. "I'm ashamed of you. It's a wonder you didn't hurt yourselves. I hate to think of what the consequences might have been. Give me those keys, Sarah."

"Aw," said Sarah, laying the keys in Aunt Mamie D.'s hand.

"Aw, don't tell on us," said Elise, as they ran into the house.

"Aw, I can't wait," said Brother, and he lost his balance and fell off the banister into the sweet white climbing rose at the corner of the high porch. He set up a howl like he was dying. Otis, Jr., took a flying leap and landed clear of him on the grass. Then he got up and started pulling thorns out of Brother's arms and shoulders.

"Brother," stormed Aunt Mamie D., "I told you to wear a shirt. Now look at you! All bloody!"

Brother screamed, "Blood? Blood?" He acted as wild as he did the day Mrs. Burris' fox terrier bit him.

I plucked a thorn Otis, Jr., had missed on his jaw.

"Come in the house and let me wash you. Get some iodine, Sister."

"No!" screamed Brother, "No! Not iodine! We don't use iodine!"

"But we have to do something, honey. You are all scratched up! You'll get blood poisoning."

Blood poisoning! Brother had nearly died with double pneumonia last winter. He could come down with anything. I hoped Mama would get home in time to see him alive.

Brother was close to having a fit. "It burns," he cried hoarsely. "Mama uses mercurochrome on me."

"Go get something, Sister." Aunt Mamie D. sounded reckless as she took Brother's hand.

"Ow," he yelled. "There's still one in my hand," and his voice broke again, and tears welled up and spilled over. He was called a beautiful and irresistible child.

Otis, Jr., followed me to Mama's medicine cabinet. "We should of stayed in the treehouse," he said to himself.

"Wipe your feet," said Aunt Mamie D. to all of us.

"We should of stayed in the treehouse," Otis, Jr., said again. "You know what he came all the way up to the house for?"

"What?"

"Just to take a leak. He could of gone out there. Didn't even need to climb down. He could of stood there and hit every one of Buster Brister's hounds in the eye just like that. But he was afraid Aunt What's-her-name would see him."

I said, "She wouldn't have seen him if he'd gone on the other side of the tree."

"I know it, but he never did go," said Otis, Jr. "He still hasn't gone. He forgot all about it when he ran out there to watch Sarah and Lizzy. Boy!"

Aunt Mamie D. sat on the back porch settee with Brother standing between her soft knees. Every time she painted another red spot on him he scrunched up and yelled, "Ouch!" When she got through he went and looked at himself in the hall mirror. He twisted and turned to see himself all over. "Look at that, Otis," he said seriously. "That old rose tore me up."

"You should of gone out in the back," said Otis, Jr., and when he said that, Brother flew to the bathroom.

Aunt Mamie D. leaned back and began to relax on the settee. Then she sat up again. "Where are your big sisters? They're mighty quiet." Worry had returned to her face.

"They're upstairs like you told them," I said. "Are you going to tell on them for backing Daddy's car out?"

"Oh, I don't know. I just don't know. I'll speak to the Lord about it. Sometimes that is all in this world there is to do." She sighed and looked at the clock. "Oh, mercy! The cake!" And she trotted into the kitchen and opened the oven. "Get me a straw out of the broom, Sister." She poked the back end of the straw into one of the layers. "I do believe they are all right. I completely lost track of time. Thank the good Lord. We don't need to lose three good layers of jam cake." And she took them out using her apron and a towel. After she shut the oven door she began beating the sweet syrup into the egg-whites and we iced the cake. She left me to scrape out the icing bowl while she went back to the porch. She sat down hard on the settee. "Whew!" she breathed. "Mercy on us." When the phone rang she said, "Will you get that, honey? I'm just not used to so much activity." She waved her hand toward the hall, exhausted.

The Lord was answering her prayers. "It was Mrs. Holmes," I told her. "They're coming early, Aunt Mamie D."

"What's that?" she said, like she was at last getting some good news.

"The Holmeses are ready early. They are coming on by for Sarah and Lizzy." I ran up the stairs. "Hey, Sarah! The Holmeses are getting off early. Are you all ready?" They had all three of their locks on the door. They must be smoking.

The instant Elise opened the door I said, "I smell your cigarettes."

She laughed and left the door open. "Come on in, snoop. Let's see you find one."

"I heard you flush them down the toilet."

Sarah made out like she was growling at me, but she laughed. "When?"

"When what?"

"When are they coming, dummy?"

I said, "They're on their way. I wish I was going."

"Well, you can't. Nobody allowed under fourteen. Lizzy will be the youngest one."

Elise said, "You don't have to wait but five years."

We all ran down the stairs. They hugged and kissed Aunt Mamie D. "Don't be mad at us," said Sarah.

"And don't tell on us," said Elise. "We didn't hurt anything."

"Bye, Brother," they called out the back door. Mr. Holmes was already carrying their things to the car in front of the house. Both of my sisters kissed me. "Goodbye, Sister," said Sarah. "Behave yourself."

"Too bad your sisters missed the cake," said Aunt Mamie D. later in the kitchen. She gave us all tunafish sandwiches and iced tea with lemon and mint for lunch. We heard the sound of two hammers out of rhythm through the afternoon.

The only other sounds were Buster Brister's hounds howling when a freight train came through town. Even before you heard the train whistle, one hound would bawl out and hold his note till the whistle blew. Then all the hounds would chime in with their wailing—about a dozen beagles and other hounds, stretching their necks in chorus till the train was gone. Then they shook their long ears and rattled their collars and skulked down in the dust again.

Buster's dog yard was along our back fence, and the treehouse was taking shape on two low fat mulberry branches that reached out over the hounds. Aunt Mamie D. saw this when she took lemonade to Brother and Otis, Jr., in the afternoon.

"Goodness sakes, Brother. Suppose one of you fell out of your tree. Aren't you afraid of all those dogs?"

"Naw," said Brother.

"Naw," said Otis, Jr.

"What!"

"No ma'am," they said together.

"Well, that's better," said Aunt Mamie D.

"But we ain't going to fall, Aunt Mamie D.," said Brother. "These fat limbs are too wide."

"How do you like our house?" said Brother to me, jumping down in front of me. He took me by surprise. I wasn't used to him asking me such a respectful question.

"You've done real well on those first two boards up there," I said. "Why are you all so slow?" This made Brother mad as a wet hen.

"I'd like to see you get those two long, huge boards way up there and nailed down, you're so smart."

"Can I come up?"

"Naw, you sure can't."

"No girls allowed, huh Brother." And Otis, Jr., laughed so loud I figured his mother could hear him two doors down.

Aunt Mamie D. and I left them drinking from tall glasses. "I know good and well they are going to fall in that dog yard," she said when we went inside. But they did not.

Aunt Mamie D. sat on the back porch and embroidered the rest of the afternoon. She could embroider the prettiest monograms anybody ever saw. Our sheets and pillowcases and napkins had Mama's initials on them that Aunt Mamie D. had done, beautiful curvy letters with curlicues on them. And could she evermore make a jam cake. She said we could have a slice with milk after supper.

Well, she made Brother come in and take a bath at five o'clock. By the time he got to the supper table he was so tired and sleepy he could hardly keep his head out of his plate. "Son, we'll excuse you to go on back to bed. I'll come out to hear your prayers." All he ever said was Now I Lay Me. But when Aunt Mamie D. went out on the sleeping porch Brother was sound asleep. She was so big on praying I thought she might wake him up. But she just pulled the sheet up over his legs.

Later I asked her if she wanted to play trees again that night. "Wild horses couldn't keep me awake tonight," she said, pulling the spread to the foot of the bed.

In my bed I decided I would play the game alone. I couldn't think of a D. I kicked the sheet off and thought E: Elm, and fell asleep.

When we waked up Tuesday it looked like rain. At eleven o'clock the clouds had darkened, and there were a few flickers of lightning, so Aunt Mamie D. went down in the back and sent Otis, Jr., home and made Brother come in. He didn't want to, but after a while he quit fuming, and we got out the box of cut-and-paste stuff from the window seat in Mama's room and he made some boats and I cut out snowflakes. He lined up all his boats on the rug and tied them together. "We'll take them out to the fish pool when the sun comes out," he said.

I was cutting another snowflake when a big stab of lightning flashed through the house. Aunt Mamie D. came running.

"Sister! Drop those metal scissors, instantly." I dropped them like a hot potato. "Don't you know that metal draws lightning, child? Now don't pick them up while this lightning keeps up." And she edged them far away from me with her toe.

Brother reached over and pulled the silver barette out of my hair. "Look at this, Aunt Mamie D. Will this kill her?" While he held it another big flash hit the room followed by a crash of thunder, and Aunt Mamie D. screamed. Her nervousness didn't surprise me too much, because Mama had a fear of weather. She didn't scream, but she made us sit in the room with her and be quiet while she sat up tense and straight, clutching her hands on her knees and waiting for the next streak of lightning. But I could see that poor Aunt Mamie D.

was terrified. And the storm was really whipping up. It was raining hard.

When she went to pull the draperies, another big flash cut through the room, and she ran into the hall. I began to get scared when I saw the terror in her eyes. As soon as the next flash was over I ran and pulled the curtains to. But Mama had the summer pongees up, and they didn't keep much out.

Brother said, "Gollee, Aunt Mamie D., why don't you get in Mama's bed and cover your eyes up with the pillow so you can't see what's happening." Then the wind began to get high, whipping the tops of the big oaks like they were nothing, and shrubbery was brushing against the wood walls of the house. A shutter had come loose and was slapping the dining room window, and the rain was beating the glass so hard we couldn't see out.

"Pow!" yelled Brother after the next flash and roar, and we both grabbed Aunt Mamie D.'s fat little legs. For a moment she stood there with her arms around our shoulders, staring at the window.

"What is the Lord going to do to us?" she whispered. Then she pulled away from us and brought Mama's bench from under the vanity. She set it on the back side of the high bed. "Quick, children," she said, "kneel down here. Be quick!" And she pulled us down to our knees and made an altar out of Mama's cane-seat bench. And while the storm raged with all its might, she prayed, "Oh Lord, have mercy on us. Spare these poor children. Don't let harm come to my dead sister's grandchildren." She squinched her eyes tight against the next flash and pulled our heads down to the bench when the thunder roared. Looking down through the little holes in the cane I studied the pattern in the rug and wondered why she said "my sister's grandchildren." But that was her point of view, and in all that excitement I felt more like I had really had a grandmother than I ever had before. She had died before I was born.

Brother and I might have been more frightened if we had

not been so caught up in Aunt Mamie D.'s drama. We looked up at her in her prayerful position, and we looked at each other. Brother leaned closer to me and whispered, "Do you think we ought to cry, maybe?" I shook my head no, so he said, "Aw, come on, Aunt Mamie D. He ain't gonna let nothing happen to us."

Aunt Mamie D. stroked his blond head and was saying, "You precious child," when Daddy's biggest pecan tree crashed against the back of the house. Aunt Mamie D. screamed and we screamed, and we all ran into the back hall and could see the back porch windows were covered with the treetop, wet leaves plastered to glass.

"What's happening?" said Brother.

"The world's coming to an end," I said.

"Lord have mercy!" said Aunt Mamie D. And her face was white and all her wrinkles had gotten deeper, and her hair was standing out from her head. We just stood there against the wall till she said, "Get away from the telephone!" and she dragged us back into Mama's room. And we stood there by the bench. I figured she wanted to pray some more, so I knelt down at the bench again, but I was the only one, so I got up.

"Listen," said Brother, his blue eyes wide. The wind had died down. The lightning had become a small flicker.

"It's going away," I said. And Aunt Mamie D. sort of jumped up and threw herself across Mama's bed and said, "Oh, children, we're saved. We're saved." I patted her chubby ankle, which was sticking out toward me. I didn't know what else to do. And Brother crawled up on the bed and patted her shoulder. "Don't be afraid anymore, Aunt Mamie D. It's all going away. Look how light the room is now. We ain't going to get blown away, and the lightning ain't striking anymore."

I let him alone about *ain't*. The storm had just about disappeared. We went out on the back porch, and we couldn't see through the packed pecan leaves against the windows, so we went into the kitchen. The whole tree was blown over and the roots had brought up a huge circle of dirt and brought part of

Buster Brister's fence with it, and his hound dogs were running every which way in our backyard. Over their yapping,
Aunt Mamie D. said, "What else can happen?" But I could see
she wasn't nearly as upset about the dogs or even the tree now
that we weren't going to be blown to kingdom come or struck
by lightning. The sun came out and we went out on the front
porch and saw everything gleaming wet and sparkling. It
smelled good and washed up like it always does after a storm.

Buster Brister came around the side of the house, hollering
after his dogs. He lifted his hat to Aunt Mamie D. and told her
he was sorry about the dogs and that he'd have somebody
come with a chain saw and cut the pecan tree away from the
back of the house.

"Do you think we ought to call Daddy?" I asked him. I
wanted to tell him and Mama so bad.

"When will they be back?" said Buster.

"Friday," said Aunt Mamie D. quickly.

"Naw'm. I wouldn't call him if he's coming home that
soon. It'd just bother him, mess up his drive home. We'll clear
things up around the house. Nothing is serious except the
tree." His hounds began collecting around him, barking,
jumping up at him. He shrieked a loud whistle and they
quieted down and followed him back through our lot. In no
time he had his fence back up and his hounds inside.

Aunt Mamie D. wouldn't let us go outside while the men
with the saw trimmed the top out of the pecan tree, so Otis,
Jr., came up and the three of us sat at the kitchen table and ate
jam cake and watched while the saw whined and screamed
through the limbs of Daddy's big fine papershell he was so
proud of. He was going to be sad about that. Otis, Jr., said he
was glad it wasn't the mulberry. But Otis, Jr., didn't know a
good papershell pecan tree was worth a hundred times his and
Brother's squatty old mulberry.

Brother said, "Too bad Sarah and Lizzy missed this." Aunt
Mamie D. caught her breath, and I knew she was glad they
weren't there. They just made her nervous. That was plain.

Things stayed pretty quiet after the storm. We went to prayer meeting Wednesday night, and Aunt Mamie D. had a good time praying and singing hymns with everybody else, and all the congregation and the preacher were sweet to her. Thursday, Otis, Jr.'s mother came up and sat on the front porch with us while we shelled butterbeans for supper. We gave her some jam cake. Thursday it rained again, but nothing drastic. Friday morning we walked down to the grocery store. Aunt Mamie D. made us hold her hands all the way down and all the way back so we wouldn't be hit by a car. We stopped by the library, and I got a fresh Nancy Drew.

Friday night Mama and Daddy called us. They were in Jackson at the Edwards House and decided they were too tired to drive the rest of the way. They talked to me first because I answered the phone.

"How's everything at home, Sister?" Mama wanted to know.

"Just fine," I said.

When Aunt Mamie D. got on she said we'd been just as sweet as two children could be.

Brother said, "What did you bring me?"

Since it was her last night, I slept with Aunt Mamie D., and we played naming flowers this time. She knew so many more than I did, I didn't have such a good time. But we named all the way to the L's before she began to get sleepy. "Larkspur," I said, and she didn't answer.

The Birthday Party

As THEY PASSED Crash Landing, Kate looked at her watch. Leaving New Orleans, she liked to time herself crossing the causeway, and the little prop plane suspended in a timeless nosedive over the disco joint always reminded her. The problem was that she usually forgot to look at her watch when she got to the north side of Lake Pontchartrain.

The morning had started out dismal, but the fog was no longer too dense for safe driving, and Kate could see white-caps snapping at the shallow lake's choppy surface, gulls skimming high and low, now camouflaged against the pale sky, now sharply white against the slate water. A gull lay on the lane divider, its body flattened, but its wings flying up in the wake of speeding automobiles that fled the city.

The "new" causeway swept off ahead for twenty-four miles. Parallel traffic going into New Orleans zipped past a few yards away on the "old" causeway, its more open railing whipping by like iron and concrete hemstitching. Ahead, the two bridges seemed to merge at a point far above an indistinct horizon.

Jack drove the Datsun sedan, one hand relaxed over the lower arc of the steering wheel, his profile immobile. The wheels clicked along over the lines in the pavement, and Kate saw the blue call boxes as they flashed by. Under each blue box was a smaller yellow box labeled HELP. At box 110 they left Jefferson Parish and entered St. Tammany.

The black-green pine fringe on the north shore became visible, and sails of small boats jutted up like shark fins. The air was clearing rapidly, and by the time Jack turned off the bridge toward Mandeville, the sun had burned the fog away. The day was becoming brilliant. Good, thought Kate. Surely her father's birthday could be a happier celebration on a beautiful day.

Benjamin popped his jaw hollowly, and when Kate looked over her shoulder at him, smiling, he grinned back at her. "I'm really getting this down, Mom. Listen." He put his middle finger into his cheek and popped it out again. "Wow, wait'll Grandaddy hears that. He taught me how." He made the noise again. "Mom?"

"Yes, Benjamin."

"Did you remember that it was Granddaddy who taught me?"

"Oh. Yes, I remember that."

Kate wondered if her father remembered teaching Benjamin. She wondered if he remembered teaching her to tie a clove hitch and a hangman's noose and to make a Jacob's ladder with string, and a mill with string and a button, thread a worm into a bream hook. What the doctors called little strokes had wrought changes in him that she could not quite believe. His moods changed erratically. One day, she thought, when we come he might not remember anything. More likely I'll say or do something he won't forgive. He could get so angry so quickly now, with Willa and Adele, usually for something they said. Kate was fearful of forgetting to be careful, of saying something. You made mistakes when you tried too hard.

"We're almost there," she said to Benjamin. "Here, take my comb and smooth your hair. Get it back off your forehead." She passed a narrow amber comb over the back of the seat.

Jack turned right and headed down the old shell road, straddling potholes filled with milky water, toward East Lakeshore. His big dark glasses did not keep him from frowning as he confronted the glittering water of Lake

Pontchartrain. Now, back left to run along the blacktop between the lake and the comfortable old houses that looked
out over the water.

Willa's lawn, facing the lake, had a white picket fence
across the front, and a shell drive curved up to the steps of the
house and out to the road again. Five or six cars could park
under the live oak that spread almost the width of the white
clapboard raised cottage. George's nineteenth-century an-
cestor had wanted a perfect view of the lake from the high
wraparound gallery and from the ample shuttered dormers in
the steep gable. The oak now blocked some of that view of the
lake from the ends of the long gallery where there were
swings and rockers. Wicker tables with begonias, geraniums,
a few cacti. Great ferns with long arching fronds hung in
baskets over the banisters. Kate's brother-in-law sat at one
end, and her father sat at the other. Squared off, she thought.
When Jack stopped their car, a gray drape of Spanish moss lay
over the windshield, casting a shadow over the front seat.

"There he is on the porch," Benjamin shouted. "Hi,
Granddaddy!"

"Benjamin, now remember how very old Granddaddy is.
Jack . . . don't either of you say anything he'll think is dis-
respectful. Benjy, you remember to speak plainly. He's getting deaf. Don't mumble."

Jack laid his keys on the dashboard. "Looks like they've
signed a peace treaty."

"Don't jump to conclusions. Just don't . . ."

"Ah, Kate, don't be so nervous. If he's in a good humor,
okay. If he's angry with Willa and George, nothing we can do
will help or hurt. What are you afraid of? You're just too
intimidated."

"See, that's what I mean."

"Honey! Relax."

George was out of his chair, stepping spryly down the steps.

"George." Kate leaned forward and touched her cheek to
his. George held his pipe to one side and smiled through his

white moustache. "You're looking chipper, Kate, as always." And he turned to shake hands with Jack.

"Looks like you and the old gentleman have gone to your corners," Jack grinned.

"Jack." Kate's look was baleful. "Lower your voice." Jack pinched her bottom. "Dammit, Jack. Stop it." But she knew the pinch was a gesture toward lightheartedness. She started up the broad wood steps. George must have painted them for the gathering. There were smudges of dark green enamel on the grass that nestled against the first step, and the banister rail was gleaming white and felt a little sticky.

Her father sat watching them, his arthritic hands clutching the arms of the high-backed rocker as though the chair were about to become airborne. His once tall, firm body angled into the chair, brittle as a winter leaf. Now he was pushing himself up, trying to stand erect. His old panama flapped against Kate's back as he embraced her awkwardly. With his other hand he caught Benjamin by the ear. Benjamin screamed and laughed, "Granddaddy! Granddaddy! Stop it! Are you really eighty-five years old today?" He jumped around in front of his grandfather, popping his cheek.

But the old man said, "Hush. Hush, boy. You don't have to holler." Taking Kate's elbow, he smiled, his mouth caving. "Well, come on," he said. "Come on and sit down with me." He leaned on Jack as he shook his hand and turned back to the rocker. "Sit down. Sit down." He put his hat back on, pulling the brim low against the brilliant day.

Kate sat beside him wishing she had something marvelous to tell him, something that would make him put his head back and laugh one of his big guffaws strong and full of healthy mirth. Restore him somehow, if just for today.

"We had a nice drive over," she began.

"Have you sold any more articles?" He was proud of her research and writing. She knew that.

"Sorry, Daddy. Not since last spring."

Her father looked disappointed. "She'll have to get busy,"

he said to Jack. His blue eyes, bright under white brows, looked across the blue hydrangeas growing against the picket fence, and far out over the blue and silver water. Kate looked from him to the rufous-sided towhee that scratched near the hydrangeas, its claws scattering bits of mulch and fine black dirt.

"The research is slow, Daddy . . ." She was relieved to see her sister come out the screened door. Willa was handsome, stylish, even in a flowered apron that hung a little longer than her yellow linen bermudas.

"Well, I just said to myself, 'It's time those McLeans are getting here.' Hello, Darling. Hmmmm! How're things in that filthy city? It's kissy time, Benjamin. Oh, Lord, so you've outgrown kissy time with Aunt Willa. Jack! You look marvelous. Marvelous." The old man groaned and turned away.

So, thought Kate, it's to be an edgy day. She wished her father would not forget how close he and Willa had been. He used to say, "Willa can handle an automobile as well as any man. She's the best woman driver I ever saw." Kate had regarded that oft-repeated statement a great compliment for a father to pay his daughter. Back then, it was.

"Just wait till you see this turkey I have in the kitchen. And cornbread dressing I cooked just the way Granddaddy likes it, Benjamin, full of sage." Willa happily beamed on all of them for a moment. Then she lowered her voice and motioned to Kate, "Come on in." Kate followed her down the wide hall, saying, "The hydrangeas are bluer than ever. Do you still put rusty nails around them to make them such a deep shade?" In the kitchen, she said, "How's everything going? He seems to be in good spirits."

"Oh, he is right now. And maybe he will be all day. He's so glad you're here. I wonder if the Allens will show up. Adele will probably call just at dinnertime and say she got up too late." Willa opened the oven. "Look at that, I wish you would. Now I ask you, isn't that the most gorgeous golden brown bird you ever laid your two eyes on? Benjamin? Where's Benjy? I wanted him to see this thing."

She closed the oven and looked unhappy. "It'll probably taste awful. Heaven knows I don't know how to cook a turkey. And with Daddy watching over every move I make in here, telling me what to do, I've nearly had a stroke. You just don't know. You cannot know, Kate. You don't live with this day after day." She was hurriedly rubbing a large damp cloth over the Formica counter.

"Now, let's see," she muttered to herself, "the turkey, the dressing, gravy, asparagus casserole, black cherry salad. Oh, God! Katey, honey, will you be a love and grate that block of frozen cream cheese for the salad? The rolls are buttered." She turned abruptly and opened the screened door to the side porch. "George!" she called, "have you made the bloody marys?" Then, "Kate, I know you don't like bloody marys; you can have something else."

"Blood's okay," said Kate, raking the hard white cheese over the grater. "Are you glad you took early retirement, Willa?"

Willa dropped the cloth over the spigot between the sinks. "Oh, I suppose so. I had to slow down. And what do you mean 'early retirement'? I worked twenty-seven years at that ad agency. I'll have to admit that I'm about to lose my mind, now, here with two old men. I'll probably have a stroke right there—fall flat on my face." She pointed to the floor just inside the dining room. Kate turned to look at the dark pine of the floor, half expecting to see Willa's legs across the threshold, feet in the kitchen.

"I pledge you my word that this is the best dressing I ever put in my mouth. Doesn't it smell divine?" She pulled the wrinkled foil back over the roasting pan, sealing the edges with her pot holders. "If he doesn't like that, there's no pleasing him." The kitchen was filled with steamy rich odors of turkey, onion, celery, cornbread.

"He does love turkey and dressing, and you're right, that

looks gorgeous." Kate looked hungrily at the brown skin of the turkey, golden juices seeping from the breast.

Willa straightened. "Wasn't that a car door?" Kate followed her to the front hall.

Adele's husband had parked under the oak, and he was helping her from the backseat of the glistening black car. Adele stood, giving her body a quick, almost military stiffening. She wore her short white hair in a smooth pageboy, as she had at eighteen when it was pale gold. "I never change my hairdo or my hemline," she liked to say.

As she watched Adele come up the dark green steps, Kate felt her eyelids close like a slow shutter. Adele wore beige jodhpurs, brown ankle boots, a cream cashmere turtleneck sweater, and a tightly belted, but open, trench coat that hung below midcalf. She tugged at the fingers of her white kid gloves, clenched her teeth on her long ivory cigarette holder, and tilted her head up sharply so her big black sunglasses would not slip farther down on her nose while she protested to her husband that he had not pulled the car far enough under the tree.

Kate wondered whatever had happened to the pince nez that Adele wore when she first married. She could remember her eccentric-looking sister at the bridge table with the much older ladies—the *serious* bridge players—the little spectacles clipped on her nose, the silver chain pinned on her girlish shoulder. Kate had fully intended to have such glasses herself when she grew up and married.

Now Adele nodded to her father, who had not seemed to notice her arrival. She strode across the porch into the hall, toward her sisters, her slender legs moving as though she were on a long hike with miles to go yet.

"Del! It's good of you to come. How are you, Darling?" Willa bent to loosely clasp her smaller but older sister.

"Somewhat better, thank you," said Adele over her holder. "Of course I live on the precipice, as one must who is married to . . ."

"Mercy, Adele," sighed Willa, rolling her eyes toward Kate. Now Kate and Adele tapped cheeks and spectacles as Harrison Allen came into the hall. Kate watched Willa kiss him warmly, as though she liked him. "Hi, Harrison, here's your kissin' sister, honey. How are things in Mississippi? Adele, you look marvelous, just marvelous. You all come on in. My God, Daddy hasn't been in such a good humor in weeks. I swear, he and George got into an argument over whether to prune that fig tree by the back door last night, and I thought they might kill each other. The idea! Prune a fig tree this time of year! Harrison, the bar is where it always is. Take your coat?"

Harrison removed his beige linen coat and handed it to Willa. He murmured thanks pleasantly, smiled vaguely toward Kate as if he could not quite place her, and returned to the porch. George was holding a martini pitcher out to Harrison, grinning, and stirring with the long glass stick, "carefully, so as not to bruise the gin." Adele followed Willa down the hall as Harrison's voice drifted back after them. "Stewpid," he was saying to George. "Stewpid."

The women went into the guest room, Adele clutching her arms against her private chill. She said in a low voice, "When you are married to a madman, you are forced into strange behavior—I should say forced into behavior that *appears* strange to others who just don't *know.* Harrison Allen keeps his car freezing cold, so that when I'm forced to ride with him I must swathe myself warmly summer and winter." She shivered, still clutching her arms. The sunburst brooch of diamonds hanging on a heavy chain around her neck was anchored to the sweater. She laid her brown leather handbag and a pair of binoculars on Willa's crocheted bedspread.

"Your pin looks beautiful," Kate said from the door.

"Thank you, Kate." Adele plucked the spent cigarette from her holder. "I had to have it redesigned, as you no doubt know. It was years ago. Harrison gave it to me in the most hideous black enamel setting. Ugh!"

"Well, it looks good, now."

Adele's eyes darted from Willa to Kate and back to Willa, where her gaze settled briefly through the smoke. "I want to tell you all that I'm thinking of engaging Louis Nizer," she said. "Have you read his book?"

"Which one? He's written more than one," said Willa, who read practically everything.

"I haven't any idea," said Kate.

Keeping her voice low and continuing to look from one sister to the other, Adele said, "I really believe Nizer could get a divorce for me. I have tried to consult all the best lawyers in the county, and none of them will represent me. I simply cannot understand it. All of them have known me all my life. Mr. Hub Curtin never even returned my call. And after everything Daddy did for that brother of his. But you all listen to me. Nizer hates men! He knows what rotters they are. I believe he would represent me if he heard my story. Can't you just see me marching into the courthouse at home with Louis Nizer at my side? Then those country lawyers would show up! Every lawyer in Mississippi would be there."

"But his fee would be enormous," said Kate. "Louis Nizer? Good grief, Adele. And if you did divorce Harrison, where would . . ."

"These tacky earrings would pay a lawyer. I'm dead serious, Kate. You don't know what I've put up with from Harrison. Ask Willa. She knows. You're too young to remember everything." Adele flicked her lighter and held it out before herself like a lamp while she talked. "And where will I live? I've thought about that so long! I'll have a little *pensione* in Paris part of the year. And other times a place in Santa Barbara, maybe. I saw a special on Santa Barbara the other night on educational TV. It is now one of the few places in this whole country still fit for human habitation." Kate was glad Jack couldn't hear.

Nevertheless, she maneuvered Adele back to the porch. "Let's go talk with Daddy. He wants to see you." When she said it Kate was hit with her own sense of unreality. Their father never wanted to talk with Adele. When she wasn't present he liked to talk about her—how smart she was, how much money she had wasted when he sent her away to college, like it was yesterday. And he often said she had the best-looking legs "of all you girls." But face-to-face with Adele he didn't have an ounce of patience with her "foolishness."

Benjamin sat on the floor beside his grandfather's chair. The old man's hand rested upon the boy's head. "You ought to get some of that hair cut off, son," he was saying, as he looked at Adele's jodhpurs. "You look like a girl, just like your mama looked when she was nine. Isn't that about how old you are? You don't want to look like a girl, do you?"

Adele put out her hand. "How are you, Daddy?" she said. "Please don't get up." He had half made a gesture of rising.

"Well, Miss, did you tether your horse at the hitching post? Ask your Aunt Del where she tied up, Ben." Kate winced.

Benjamin studied his aunt's clothes, but he didn't laugh. He looked at his mother. Adele looked perplexed and her chin came out slightly. She offered her father a cigarette from her open case. She rasped a flame from her gold lighter and held it politely at the end of the cigarette until the old man got a light. Then she excused herself and walked down the steps and around into the side yard where the pecan and fig trees grew.

The brothers-in-law had settled at the other end of the long porch, near the bar. They sat talking, comfortable-looking in their Daks and Gants and Ballys, laughing quietly, sipping drinks. Harrison had his heel on the swing's edge, his wrist hung over his knee, martini glass tilting in his hand. George slumped in a canvas chair, his ankles crossed on the banister. Jack, looking less settled in, leaned against the post. He slapped at the back of his neck, though Kate had seen no mosquitoes or gnats.

"Sit down, Kate," said her father. "I've been wanting to talk to you about something." She sat, knowing he would now tell her again how he had arranged his affairs. He was ready to die. Waiting. He sat forward on the edge of the rocker, his eyes studying her eyes in a way that moved her. Then he laid one long hand, palm up, on his knee, and with the forefinger of his other hand he began to tap out his points.

"Now, listen to me. I've got everything fixed. There is no need for a will. I've converted everything . . . You aren't paying attention to me."

"Of course I am, Daddy." She smiled at him. Then she tapped his knee and laughed warmly, teasingly, "Go on."

He laid his head back and coughed out a laugh. "I guess I've told you all this before," he said between strangling coughs, his eyes watering. When she was little he used to put a black watermelon seed over one tooth and smile at her. They would laugh. He could be a very funny man. Once he played the mother of the bride in a charity womanless wedding that was held down in the courthouse. He stole the show in Mrs. Beulah Whittington's yellow organza dress, the great silk cabbage rose on his wide-brimmed leghorn hat bobbing as he wailed out the sorrow of the mother giving up her daughter.

"I've willed my body to science."

"For crying out loud, Daddy. You're kidding me."

"I am not kidding. Why would I kid about a thing like that? I've signed papers. Get Willa to show you."

Willa loomed by Kate's chair. "Get Willa to show you what?"

"It's not that I don't believe it . . ." She didn't want to hear about it. Not today. Her eyes slid along the porch rail, half noting the knicks and scars smoothed by many a coat of white paint. "Well, I don't know . . . of course . . . yes, it is a good thing to do . . . of course . . ."

"I think it's a splendid gesture," said Willa, taking a noisy suck on her bourbon. She rattled her ice and went back into the house.

"Liquorheads," muttered the old man. "You don't know

what I put up with. You don't know because you hardly ever come to see me anymore."

"Oh, Daddy."

"Don't 'oh, Daddy' me. The greatest mistake I ever made was selling my home in Mississippi and moving down here. Sometimes I think I'll just pack up and go back."

"Where would you go?" It wasn't a fair response.

"That's just it. There's no place to go now that I've sold my place. And every one of my old friends is dead now. Did Willa tell you Dwight Thompson died last week?"

"Mr. Dwight? Oh, no." Kate felt a flash of memories of her father's longtime fishing friend, a country banker, father of her own oldest friend. She laid her hand on his, and he looked down at them. His ravaged old face bore little resemblance to the face Kate would remember when she got back to New Orleans. It was always like that. She would go back to seeing him as he had been to her. He would become that other person, surely partly imagined. Strong and in control. In need of no one, needed by everyone. Running everything. But full of fun if you let him have his own way.

"Really, Daddy, Willa has made you comfortable here. They seem to do everything they can. You have that lovely room up there overlooking the lake, her beautiful yard."

He shifted restlessly in the chair. "You just don't know what you're talking about."

"Well, I thought you all seemed to be getting along . . ." Her voice trailed off. Adele came up the steps.

"I just saw an ivory-billed woodpecker in that tall pine down by the road at the back," she said casually as she lifted the binocular strap from her neck.

"Young lady, you saw no such thing," said her father. "That is a pileated. You know good and well that nobody's seen an ivory bill around here in half a century." Kate escaped. She had heard the ivory-bill dialogue before. Also the passenger pigeon. A bird dispute was one sure way to get his attention,

but it was a strange ploy for Adele, who knew more about
birds than all of them put together.

Kate found Willa leaning against the highboy in her bedroom. "I hear him complaining out there." She waved her
glass in a half circle. "Kate! If you knew what this is doing to
me. Look at my house. Just look at it! Every square inch is
filled—look at those bookcases in my hall. Six of them!
Would you like to look into the Harvard Classics? Compton's
encyclopedia? Bulwer-Lytton? He'll never open a one of them
again. Bret Harte! They have no business here. Every room
has something useless crowded into it. Boxes under the beds.
And you just don't know what it's like living with two old
men who don't speak half the time, and when they do, it's
only to fuss. I'm in the middle. I tell George, 'Look at Adele up
there. She's not about to be bothered.' And you can't keep
him."

"I could and I would. But you know he can't last three days
in New Orleans. And it's just a fact that he can't last happily
with any of us more than a day or so."

"Even you, his baby," said Willa without rancor.

"Even me." She paused, feeling the smooth edges of the
bedpost. "Let's just ask him if he'd like to spend part of the
time in a good—a really nice—home for old folks."

"No. No. I can't. I can't do it. I can't believe you could
seriously suggest that we put Daddy in a home. And the irony
of him spending everything he has on one of those expensive
places . . . Kate, you're not thinking straight. Or very hu-
manely, either. You see, that's the difference in our ages. You
get a few more years on you, and you won't talk so glibly
about *homes.*"

"I didn't mean to sound glib, but things don't seem to be
working out like you expected when you moved him down
here. Heaven knows I've wondered if he actually might enjoy
being among other old people."

"I doubt it. George is old," she snapped. "He and Daddy will
both outlive me. I spend my days and nights trying to keep

peace between them. I'm going to fall flat on my face right on that floor with a stroke. Just remember I said that, you and Adele both. I know my blood pressure is probably 250 over 150 right this minute."

Kate said, "Look, Jack hid the birthday cake in the pantry. It's not beautiful, but it's the best Betty Crocker and I can do. I have candles, too. I think it will taste kind of good. I put some of those pecans you shelled for me on the top."

"Let me get half a drink before I serve."

Kate followed Willa to the porch and fixed herself a Scotch and soda with a twist of lemon. Adele asked for a little plain soda on ice, adding quietly, "It will probably make me break out, but everybody else is drinking something."

They joined their father, who was scolding Benjamin for swinging too high and kicking the rocking chair. Then the old man turned his attention to Adele.

"I'm leaving my body to science," he said. Adele looked startled. She blinked but said nothing. "Science is everything," he went on. "I've got all those books in there on science, and I've read them all. It's possible to believe in the Bible and evolution, too. Science is easier to prove, but I'd hate to get to the end of the row not believing the Bible and find out it was all true. Then I'd be up the creek without a paddle." He winked at Benjamin.

"Granddaddy, you say the funniest things. Mom, did you hear what he said?"

Kate's laugh was strained. "Certainly I hear him, Benjamin." She looked out past Willa's fern baskets twisting slowly to the left, then to the right, wagging their long green fronds to some mysterious rhythm conspired between the lake breeze and the ceiling fans. She watched the small boats on the lake—their sails bobbing like toys. This was the best of early summer days—the soft and salty air. They couldn't last much longer, she thought. Long, hot, humid midsummer days became oppressive. They sapped the energy. Her father did not suffer from the heat. "My blood is old and thin," he

had told her more than once. He had told her as often that
he'd been middle-aged when she was born, long after the
others, that everyone thought he wanted a son, but he hadn't,
he said. "You came late and kept me and your mother young."
Death had kept her mother young forever, younger than
Adele and Willa were now.

Jack came over and offered to sweeten drinks as the old man
was getting to his feet. "I think I'll fix me a little toddy," he
said, and walked toward the bar on the white wicker table.

"Can I fix it for you, Mr. Ben?"

"No thanks, Jack. I can get it." He bent over to pour the
bourbon, then walked around the side porch to the kitchen.

Adele took a filter from her handbag and replaced the one in
her holder. Then she lighted a cigarette and watched it red-
den, looking almost cross-eyed, at the tip for a moment. "I
wish we could play Botticelli," she said. "I guess there's not
time, now. I had the best time I've had in years that night I
played at your house. I am completely starved for intellectual companionship."

"Why don't you get some of your friends at home together
to play. There's nothing to it, you know."

"Kate! You know none of my friends have sense enough to
play that game. You had Savonarola that night and I had . . ."

"You had Pearl Buck!" laughed Kate, "and nobody ever did
guess it. I remember how everybody screamed when you finally had to tell us. How about the bridge players? Anybody
who can call a hand after the bids ought to . . ."

"The bridge players are all dead, or most of them. Nursing
homes. And bridge is all they ever knew. Nobody in Middleton knows anything. And that certainly includes that rogue I
married." She opened her eyes wide and focused both again on
the end of her cigarette. She leaned closer. "I think Willa is
getting tipsy."

Kate rattled her own ice as if armor in support of Willa.
"Not really. But who could blame her?"

"Alcohol is not the answer." She sat back. "We all have our

crosses, Kate. You don't, apparently. Yet." She looked down the porch at Jack. "You will, eventually. Harrison goes into drunken rages and curses me, threatens me, Kate. You don't believe me, do you?"

"I believe you."

Adele dropped her voice. "Would you believe that he called me an ass, just this morning? An *ass*, mind you. Mama would have walked right out and gone home to Grandpa if Daddy had ever spoken disrespectfully to her. And Grandpa would have horsewhipped Daddy."

Kate kept her face straight. "How do you know Daddy didn't?"

"Didn't what?"

"Didn't treat Mama disrespectfully. Some way."

"Men didn't behave like that in her day. Not the people I come from."

Kate looked up at the waving ferns and waited.

"Kate, there is just much you don't know." Adele stopped and sneezed. "My nose never unstops. I am allergic to everything in this world. All flora; all fauna."

Their father shuffled back to his chair.

"How's the dinner coming, Granddaddy?" asked Benjamin. "I'm hungry."

"Turkey looks good, but I think the cook's tooted." He laughed and smacked his lips at Benjamin. Benjamin laughed.

"Did you hear that, Mom? He means Aunt Willa's drunk." Kate laid her hand over Benjamin's mouth and looked at her father. He cackled and settled into his chair. His iced-tea glass was dark with bourbon, and an inch of sugar drifted in the bottom like sand in an hourglass. He took a swallow and made a face, shaking his head.

"Nosirree," he said, "I don't want any fighting over what I've left when I'm gone. I've got it all fixed. Those certificates are all signed . . ."

"Are we about ready to eat, Willa?" called Jack. Kate knew he wanted to go home.

"I think Willa is about ready to serve," Kate said. "You all drink up. I'm going to see if I can help her." She went to the dining room and began to arrange trivets and trays on the sideboard. Adele was at the table refolding the napkins at each place.

"Willa," she said, "I received a thank-you note from Helen's new daughter-in-law yesterday, written in blue ink. Wouldn't Helen die! I know she must have selected the girl's stationery. It was quite appropriate. But blue ink! People just don't care anymore."

"There's no health in us, Adele," said Willa, and elbowed Kate as she put a ladle by the gravy boat. "Now, you all let me serve Daddy's plate first and get him seated. Then the rest of you can fall to. Kate, run back and get the salt and pepper shakers. He doesn't like cellars. Oh, Lord, and take that goblet away and bring him a double old-fashioned full of buttermilk." She carefully lifted slices of white meat onto her father's plate.

Adele watched Willa and their father during the seating and took a few last little puffs on her cigarette before she snuffed it out in an ashtray on a side table. Then she joined the family as they filed past the sideboard, helping themselves to dinner, murmuring compliments over the food. The men seated the women.

"Thank you, Sweetie," said Willa to Jack, raising her voice above the general chatter. "Daddy, will you please say grace?"

He bowed his head and squinted his eyes closed. "Thank Thee, oh Lord, for these Thy bountiful gifts which we are about to receive. In Jesus' name, amen." His head bobbed up, and he laid his napkin across his lap. Kate raised her head slowly, thinking that he still said *Thee* and not *You*. "Amen" echoed around the table.

"Now," smiled Willa. "What can I pass you, Daddy?"

"I'd like some cranberries, please."

"Oh, my God," she moaned, "I forgot to get cranberries.

Oh, Daddy, how could I? Will you take pepper jelly? Maybe kumquat preserves? I made them. Mayhaw?"

"No ma'am. I don't want any of that." And the old man began to pick at his dressing with his fork. "Turkey needs cranberries."

"I put lots and lots of sage in the dressing . . . just like you like it."

"Something makes it taste . . ." began Benjamin, but Kate laid her hand on his knee. He had never tasted sage.

"Everything is just lovely," said Adele. "Really, Willa, I do not know how you do it. And keep up this big house with no help." She finished with an edge of disapproval in her voice.

"The dressing is perfect, Willa," said Kate, looking toward her father. "Daddy, this giblet gravy is something else, isn't it?"

The old man cleared his throat and rubbed his napkin back and forth across his mouth. "Well, I've had aplenty. I'm going up and take a little nap," he said, getting up unsteadily.

Kate said, "Oh, wait, Daddy. I have a surprise for you. I made you a birthday cake. Let me get it before you lie down."

"What kind is it?"

"Chocolate. With fudge icing," she called, already in the kitchen. "With Willa's pecans."

"I don't eat chocolate anymore," he said, starting for the hallway. "It constipates me."

"But wait," pleaded Kate. "At least blow out the candles." She set the cake down hurriedly, and Jack was already on his feet lighting the circle of candles. Benjamin wanted to lift the cake up to his grandfather.

"Look out, boy. Look out! You'll burn the house down." But he turned and leaned over the cake. Steadying himself on the arm of his chair, he pursed his lips and blew out all the candles. Then he caught his breath and staggered back a step. Everyone at the table made a little gasp and leaned as if to catch him. But he stood looking at them now like he was recollecting who they were and why they were there. He smiled, first looking down at Benjamin, and he continued to smile weakly as he looked back around the table. "You all go on and enjoy yourselves. Eat your dinner." He sounded as though he were addressing all of them as children again. "I've got to go on up and stretch out. It was nice, Willa." He glanced her way again and gave a nod.

Kate felt her throat constrict as he started for the hall. He used to go into the big old-fashioned kitchen late at night, in his pajamas, and make dark sweet fudge, testing drops in a teacup of cold water till he knew it was done. "Pour that water out and get me a fresh cup, Kate," he would say, stirring. "It's not setting up yet." Finally he would pour the candy into a buttered platter and lay pecan halves on it so that each would be centered when he cut the squares.

Willa got up and hurried after him. "Can I help you, Daddy?"

"No ma'am. You cannot," he said, not looking back, and Kate listened to his steps slow and muffled on the stairs. Willa stood clutching her napkin with both hands for a moment before she sat down. Then the family began to eat again, cutlery rattling on china.

"Don't fret, Willa," said Jack.

"I guess I can't help it, Jack." Willa smiled at him.

Benjamin and Adele ate some cake as the others poured coffee at the sideboard and walked to the porch. Adele told Benjamin that she was allergic to chocolate and everything else, but that she would eat one little piece with him to keep him company. "I'm sorry I haven't had time to talk with you more today. You are such an intelligent boy—the kind of boy I like. Do you like to play games?"

"I don't play Botticelli, if that's what you mean, Aunt Adele," he said, licking dark icing from his lips.

"You are a nice boy," she said again and excused herself hurriedly and disappeared. She returned with her coat and handbag. She told Harrison that they must go, and she began to tell Willa and George what a wonderful time she had had. "I mean it," she said, smiling a lovely smile. "It was wonderful. I don't have many sunny hours, you know," she added to everyone on the porch. "Mine is a melancholy existence." She then strode out to the edge of the porch and began to direct her husband. "If you will just turn around and head back this way through the left gate to the road . . ."

"That's stewpid, Adele. We don't need to turn around. Why do you think they have two gates?"

"You never listen . . ." Adele pulled her trench coat up to her chin against the blast of the air-conditioner. Harrison helped her into the backseat, where she preferred to ride. The big car crunched over the shells and through the left gate.

"We'd better get on the road," Jack said to Kate exactly as he always said it. With his back to the others, he loosened his belt a notch.

"But let me help Willa first," said Kate. "It won't take long."

"Jack, how about a little B&B before you take off?" suggested George.

"I don't believe, thanks, George," said Jack, and he went back to the dining room and began to help clear the table with Kate.

But Willa said, "Kate, you all must go on and start for home. I don't want you on that causeway after dark. Somebody is killed on it every single weekend. Jack, you just can't be too careful, Sweetie." She was leading them across the porch.

"It's nowhere near dark," Kate said on the steps. "And besides . . ."

"Did you see the fog last night? No indeed, you go on now. And I want you to take that cake with you."

"But . . ."

"No buts, Kate. We'll never eat it. George and I do not touch sweets, and for God's sake, don't constipate Daddy." She laughed. "Seriously, it would just end up on the birdfeeder. Please. Take it."

"Whatever you say." Kate looked at Jack, who walked rapidly into the house. "It's been so nice, Willa," she said. "We really appreciate all the trouble you went to. I think Daddy did enjoy it. Really. I know how he acts sometimes, but . . . tell him good-bye for us. Try to get him to drive over with you for lunch one day soon."

"I will. Poor old thing. God forbid that I should ever live to be his age. I won't, of course." Kate grinned and Willa began to laugh. She laughed till she cried, leaning on Kate's shoulder. Kate looked at Jack, who had set the covered cake on the floor of the backseat. Willa became still, and Kate said, "Good-bye, Willa." The two women leaned forward and touched their cheeks together, both patting the other's shoulder.

Jack told Willa the turkey and the mayhaw jelly were delicious as he closed Kate's door and walked to his side. Benjamin pressed his nose against the back window and waved with both hands, his thumbs in his ears. Willa laughed and pointed her finger at him.

Jack drove slowly out of the yard and onto the road along Lake Pontchartrain. He pressed the button to raise Kate's window while she looked back at Willa, who stood in her yellow bermudas, waving. *Good-bye, Willa, good-bye.* George saluted jauntily from the white wicker bar and smiled through his white moustache.

Kate looked at the lake. "Look, Benjamin, the lights on the boats are coming on."

Saturday Job

DONALD REMEMBERED the first day he worked for the little old lady and the little old man. He realized later that they weren't all that old or that little. They were lots younger than his grandmother, and the woman was a good bit larger than Mamaw, who was little bitty and just getting around again after having a plastic hipbone put in. The big difference, of course, was that the little old lady was white and Mamaw was brown.

When Harvey got on with a contractor cleaning bricks, he took Donald by the house where he'd been doing yardwork, and the little old lady hired Donald on the spot, the first week in April it was. She paid four dollars an hour she said, and she expected eight hours, and she wanted her yard kept spic-and-span, mowed in the summer and raked in the fall. She wanted the beds weeded, shrubs pruned to her liking, gutters kept free of leaves, and all pavement hosed off. She would give him lunch, and he could keep a thermos of ice water outside. He could feel free to come inside to go to the bathroom and to eat.

Donald didn't know anything about flowers, but Harvey spoke out with his big snaggle-toothed smile and assured Mrs. Ward that Donald was honest and faithful, that he belonged to the Holiness Church of the Penitent Sinner, and that he would call her if ever he could not come to work.

"That is absolutely all I ask," said Mrs. Ward. "Well, Harvey," she added, "I hope this better job will mean you can buy that car you want so bad. What does it pay?"

"Minima," said Harvey, hitting his cap against his hip. "But I'll work five days a week."

The old man sniffed, and Donald figured that meant something, maybe that Harvey's job wouldn't last or that he didn't need a car. Anyway, he looked grouchy. Mrs. Ward said, "All right, Ronald, I will pick you up at eight Saturday morning. Where do you live?"

"Four-o-nine Boudreaux Alley," said Donald.

"I know where that is, behind the Hometown Meat Market. We used to buy head cheese there." She was right and she was right on time Saturday morning.

Donald stepped down off the porch and saw Mrs. Ward sweep her hand toward Mamaw's potted Easter lily on the edge. "Beautiful," she called to Mamaw, like she knew her. Mamaw beamed and rocked and waved like the Queen of England and said low, "Why, she's mighty nice, son. Now do your best for her. I never earned four dollars an hour in my life, and I washed white ladies' hair for nearly twenty years." She rocked a little bigger and waved him off.

"Don't try to get off that porch, Mamaw. I'll be back about four-thirty."

Mrs. Ward zipped her big white car through the streets like she could have driven home blindfolded, and she jabbered away about how she loved yardwork, but she couldn't do it anymore. She had something wrong with her. She talked to him about the beautiful spring weather and asked him what grade he was in and did he play basketball. "You must be about six-two," she said. "And only in the tenth grade!" Donald told her he had been sick when he was little and lost two years. And she said oh, she didn't mean to "imply" he was slow; she was just thinking of how much longer he could play basketball. "You do play, don't you?"

"No," he said, and she didn't say anymore till they got out of the car in her carport.

She showed him two storerooms where there were shovels, hoes, forks, and every kind of garden tool Donald had ever seen and then some. "We'll clean these rooms out one of these days and straighten everything up just perfect," she said, and went on showing him a riding mower, a self-propelled push mower, two Weedeaters, an electric blower, electric hedge clippers, and an electric saw. Donald leaned against a dark green louvered door and thought he might have landed an all-right job. But when he looked at the big ragged yard, he wasn't so sure. Harvey hadn't exactly been manicuring it. He felt her looking at his clothes. He looked down at his clean jeans, black-and-yellow-striped knit shirt, and Reeboks his mama had just sent him. "I don't know about those good clothes," she said. "They are going to get dirty. Next time wear old clothes and some hard-soled shoes you can push down on the shovel with." But she smiled a little. "Now, Ronald, no it's Donald, isn't it? Mr. Ward reminded me. Donald, I have these waterlilies in this fishpond," she said, and he looked into the dark pool where the reflections of tall trees made it look a hundred feet deep. The momentary illusion was terrifying, and he looked quickly back to her.

"I have this fishpond, and I love it. Just look at those beautiful fantails. But I can't clean it out anymore, and I can't get to those basins of waterlilies to give them plant pellets— fertilizer, you know. They have to have them once a month or they'll stop blooming." She pulled a long sheet of yellow paper out from under a flower pot on the table. "This is my list of work for the whole spring, all in order of priority." She began pointing to beds and to the lawn and pots and hanging baskets as she talked.

Mr. Ward came out the back door to the patio. He put one foot in a chair and stood there looking like he didn't see anything. He had on a gray suit with a vest. Polished black shoes.

"Go to the greenhouse and get the pump and the washtub," Mrs. Ward said, and as Donald walked away, "and the dipnet." He could hear Mr. Ward talking behind him, saying he didn't want that boy to use his riding mower. It had just been fixed.

And she said what was it for, that he never used it and could Donald use the hand mower, and he said no, that these boys ran too fast with it and he was tired of having it fixed and not to let him use the power saw, either. The back door slammed and Donald looked back and the little old lady was gone. Mr. Ward got into his dark blue Olds 98 and backed down the driveway.

Donald had never been in a greenhouse before, and he was surprised at how hot it was. He looked around at all the stuff. There was the pump on her workbench, a nice electric pump, and there were the dipnet and the washtub hanging on the back wall between two narrow shelves of supplies. She was going so fast with all this talk he was afraid of doing something dumb. She already thought he was dumb because he'd lost two years in school and had come to work in his good clothes. There were plenty of things in this greenhouse he didn't know beans about. Bonemeal. What was that? Vermiculite, pesticides, a spray tank, plant foods. Weird little clippers. She must have everything anybody could possibly need in here.

"Donald!" He took down the tub and the dipnet and lifted the pump off the bench. He took them to her and put them on the metal table. "Now take this pail and dip some pool water into the tub. Then dip out the fish and we'll keep them in the tub while you clean the pool. The chlorine in fresh water will kill fish. Oh, it's a heartbreaking sight to walk out here and find all your fish floating dead on top of the water. I learned that the hard way. I'll show you how to put antichlorine in the pool once you fill it up again."

After he filled the tub, Donald began chasing the fish around the curved sides of the pool. It wasn't all that easy. Those suckers could slip away like magic. "Can I take the pots out?" he asked.

"Of course. It won't hurt them to sit out a while. That parrot's feather will snap right back up." The lily pads fell over the sides of the basins. They looked like they wouldn't hold up long. Donald went back to "fishing." He caught four or five at a time and turned the net over the tub and let it flip inside out, dumping the glistening fish, which circled the tub waving their gauzy tails. Finally he counted twenty-five of them. The water in the pool was getting low, and what was left was thick and green.

Now Mrs. Ward had changed the subject. She was talking about picking up limbs and twigs that had littered the place since winter. She said he must break them up and put them in plastic bags. She had boxes full of black plastic bags in the greenhouse. Put the bags out on the curb, she said. The city had quit picking up trash that wasn't bagged. She didn't vote for the bond issue to help pay for picking up trash because the city would "misuse" the money before it was channeled to Public Works. Where she came from, the garbageman drove his truck to the backyard and picked up the trash at the back door. But that was Mississippi, this was Louisiana. They just did things differently, these south Louisiana folks.

"Come on," she said, "I want to show you what honeysuckle is so you can begin cutting it out wherever you see it, especially around the azaleas." She headed toward the far-back beds full of blooming shrubbery. "But this is after you finish the pool. The vines are strangling everything in sight," she went on kind of breathlessly. Donald knew about honeysuckle. It was on Mamaw's back fence overlooking the drainage ditch, and he liked to open the little yellow-white throat of the curly flower and taste the drops of nectar. But he didn't say anything about that to Mrs. Ward. "I used to love to cut that honeysuckle right down to the ground with those short-nosed hedge clippers, but I can't do all that anymore." They pushed through the bright flowering azalea branches, white and every shade of rose and pink, even dark, almost purple. She kicked at a thick woody vine snaking tightly around the base of an azalea. "Just look at that stuff. *Lonicera japonica.* Japanese Honeysuckle. My next-door neighbor brought that in from the country because she thought it was pretty in bloom and because it smelled good. It does smell nice, but this vine has spread all over the neighborhood. It's about ruined my azaleas. I hope you'll want a Whattaburger for lunch. I asked Mr. Ward to bring that for you at noon. French fries and a large Coke?"

"All right," said Donald. He tried to unwind a long coil of honeysuckle in the top of the big azalea. He wished she would let him finish something.

"I think the pool is about empty," she said, and they walked back to the patio, where she showed him how to use a small high-force nozzle to beat the algae off the sides of the pool. "My son and I made this pool. He dug the hole. We used hogwire for reinforcement under the concrete, then we laid these bricks around the edge together. See, he put our initials together in the bottom. And the date." She pointed her tennis shoe. "We've got some old boots in that storeroom that you can put on to step down in there. I have to go inside a little while and rest."

Donald was glad she had left him. He put on the boots and began washing down the sides of the pool. He'd never seen one of these nozzles. The sharp force of water ate through the coating of green slime on the concrete. Carefully he cut his name in script. *Donald.* Then *Ester.* When he heard Mrs. Ward coming out again he hurriedly washed out the names.

She began reading to him again from her list, talking about that bed over there, taking up that border grass, and setting out more ground cover around that birdbath. "Do you know what that plant is behind the pool?"

"No," said Donald.

"It's Asian jasmine. I love it. You see how neat it is coming right to the edge of the bricks, then the boxwoods behind that, and the nandinas just a little bit taller right behind the box, and the azaleas and so on. I'll teach you the names of everything. If you want to know them." Donald worked the water back and forth on a stubborn patch of green and then turned off the hose. The pump couldn't get the last couple of inches of water out, so he flatted the plastic bucket and bailed water into the shrubbery. Then he hosed some more. Finally, he took the nozzle off and laid the hose in the clean pool and let the water run to fill it up.

Mr. Ward brought the hamburger, and Mrs. Ward told Donald he'd probably enjoy it on the patio table. They did not have a kitchen table, and he wouldn't want to have to take his shoes off to come onto the carpet at the dinner table. Yeah. Yeah. But to go on in to wash his hands before he ate. He couldn't help smiling. Oh, hell, lady. "I'd like to eat out here." He went in and washed his hands quickly at the kitchen sink.

It was cool on the patio; it was pretty, prettier than any backyard he had ever seen. He wished Mamaw had someplace like this to sit in the shade while her hip healed, like on that comfortable-looking chaise. He rattled the ice in the huge paper cup. Well, he didn't care anything about Mrs. Ward's nandinas or her boxwoods, but four dollars an hour was four dollars an hour, and this was easy work. Crazy but easy. He took a big bite of the hamburger and leaned way back in the chair. This lady was a nutso talker, but she was okay. So was the old geezer. Something was wrong here, not just old age, he figured, but he didn't care what was bugging either one of them. If he could ignore Daddy and Miss Dorothea, as Mama called herself now, he sure didn't have to pay much attention to these crazy white folks. Clear and pure the water was slowly rising in the pool. The initials swam on the bottom, and Donald read the instructions on the antichlorine bottle.

He worked hard all afternoon cutting out honeysuckle, and at four o'clock she called him into the kitchen and gave him thirty-two dollars, and he said, "Thank you." He kicked off his Reebocks near the back door and walked in his sockfeet down the carpeted hall to the bathroom. There were white rugs on the tile floor and satin butterflies sewn on little towels by the sink. He washed his hands good and dried them on the sides of his jeans and thought how his grandmother would laugh if she could see him in here. Then Mrs. Ward knocked on the door and handed in a roll of paper towels.

She told him he had done "splendidly" when he came back to the kitchen and that Mr. Ward would pick him up next Saturday. "Your grandmother's pot plants are lovely," she added. "Colored women just have a knack with pot plants."

Mrs. Ward drove him home, talking all the way. It was like she hadn't had anybody to talk to for a year, and now she had him. He smiled inwardly. The cool air-conditioning felt good on his damp body. He looked at his reflection in the window and thought of Ester's cool smooth skin.

"Mr. Ward works too hard. He calls himself retired, but he still goes to that office very day but Sunday. Supposed to have turned it all over to the younger men, but he can't stop. I tell him, if he just had a hobby, like gardening, but he doesn't care about anything but lawyering. He's a workaholic. Some people can't stop drinking. Well Mr. Ward can't stop working. You know what an alcoholic is, I reckon, Donald. Well, Mr. Ward is a workaholic."

Oh yes, Donald knew what an alcoholic was. He thought of the years with his daddy, who sat around doing nothing while Mama stewed and finally left him and moved to Port Arthur with Roosevelt Jackson and opened her Miss Dorothea's Beauty Salon. And when Mamaw fell and broke her hip, he'd called Daddy, who lived at his girl's condo in Mobile, and he was too beery to understand that Mamaw was hurt and needed to go to the hospital. Then he called Mama in Port Arthur, and one of the hairdressers said Miss Dorothea and Roosevelt had gone to Acapulco. He had to take Mamaw to Charity Hospital, and she had to wait four hours before a doctor could see her. And Mamaw's own daughter had run off to Acapulco. "Where's that?" Mamaw kept asking him. "Where in the world is Acapulco?" she said as they rolled her into the operating room. He realized Mrs. Ward was stopping the car.

"Well, here we are," she said. And Donald said, "Thank you."

So Donald went to work for the Wards every Saturday. Mr. Ward would pick him up, bring his burger, sometimes a pizza, at noon, and sometimes walk out silently before he headed back to work. Mrs. Ward continued her garden lectures, most of the time just sitting at the metal table near the pool, watching the big goldfish as she talked to him about asparagus fern, Boston fern, holly fern, leatherleaf, and every other kind of plant anybody could ever imagine and more than he ever hoped to remember. "But ferns are my favorites," she said. And one day she brought out a book called *Ferns of Kentucky* and explained that it could have been called ferns of Louisiana since you could find most of them in Louisiana. "Do you find any of this to be interesting?" she said.

"Well—yes ma'am," said Donald, realizing he was on the edge of being sassy. "Yes," he added. "They're sure pretty. Mamaw had some pretty ones like that," he said, pointing to one of her big baskets of Boston fern, "but they dried up and died while she was getting over her hip."

"Oh, oh. Somebody neglected to water them for her." And she closed *Ferns of Kentucky.* Oh, oh was right. He should have kept his mouth shut. He'd had enough to do while his grandmother was laid up. More than ferns got neglected, and he'd learned how much Mamaw did for both of them.

On the first Saturday in August, Mrs. Ward raised him fifty cents an hour and instead of the burger she gave him a bowl of crawfish bisque she had made herself, a green salad, and french bread. Harvey showed up while he was sitting at the patio table finishing up his food.

"You got a raise? That's good, man. I got laid off last night. You planning on staying here?"

"Sure," said Donald. "Right on after school starts. I figured you gave it up for good. Right?"

"Oh, sure, Brother. You giving 10 percent to the Holinesses?"

"I will, now." He hadn't thought of such a thing, and he wasn't at all sure that he would do it. "Why'd they lay you off the job?"

"Boss cussed me, and I quit was the way it was. Preacher told us to shun foul language." Harvey's eyes were round and serious. "Man cussed me, man!"

"You kidding me? You mean to tell me you just walked off a five-day-a-week job because the man cussed you? Hell. How you going to pay for your car? You losing that car, Harvey, such as it is."

"Now you cussing. I just made a payment, and that gives me a whole month to get another job."

"Well, you don't think this job would be enough to buy a car, do you? Ain't no work in Louisiana, now. You crazy."

"Naw. I don't want you to give this job back to me. I just wondered, that's all. For all I knew, you might've been about to quit. You like them here?"

"They're okay," said Donald, sopping up the last puddle of red bisque with an arc of crust. "The old lady talks my head off, and the old man ain't so friendly, but they're okay." He grinned. "He lets me use all the power tools now, and she brings out ice water in a thermos and a Coke. They got good tools to work with . . . that wheelbarrow's rusted through, I guess they know."

"Well, I gotta go," said Harvey, and he got up and walked down the driveway. In a moment Donald heard the engine of the big old Chrysler roar into uneasy action and backfire as Harvey drove down the shady street.

There wasn't any point in trying to tell Harvey he hadn't been born again. He'd never hear the end of it. The Holiness preacher was okay. He did a lot to help boys who had been in some kind of trouble or who just weren't too smart, like Harvey. It wasn't that Donald didn't believe in God. He wouldn't argue with that. But born again? Shoot.

The next Saturday Mrs. Ward came out for only a few minutes, and since Donald was almost to the end of her list, he figured she was leaving him to "maintain the status quo," as she called it. Before she went in she said, "You've got this place looking splendid, Donald. I used to could do anything you've done, but I just can't do anything anymore. Oh, I used to be a wheelhorse. And I expect to be again." She started slowly back to the door and turned around. "I've ordered myself some lovely green rubber boots, and I mean to step down into the pool with you next time we clean it out." Donald had quit wondering what was wrong with her. He went home with his money that afternoon and gave it to his grandmother, who handed some of it back to him and as always asked him questions about the Wards.

"They're good Christian people, Donald," she said, looking proudly at the sturdy hydrangea she'd rooted from the cutting Mrs. Ward had sent her. "I want you to stay with them till you graduate. That's a good clean wholesome atmosphere for you on Saturdays. Keeps you out of trouble."

Donald's jaw tightened. He hoped she wouldn't say anything about him and Ester being caught smoking pot in the Pizza Park Inn parking lot. That's when she told him he could live with her and go to school in Ste. Marie only if he promised her he would never touch any more "merry warner" or have anything to do with Ester. And he hadn't had any more pot. He didn't want it, and he didn't want to live with Mama or Daddy or to run back and forth between Mobile and Port Arthur. Ester was something else. She wasn't bad, and he was careful, and oh, she was so . . . He sighed.

"You hear me, son?"

"Sure, Mamaw. Don't worry about that. I ain't going . . ."

"They're good . . ."

"I know it, Mamaw, but I don't want to be no white lady's yardboy forever. Next year I'll be eighteen and I'll try to get a real job, maybe with a house contractor or at one of the plants."

"You mean like Harvey? Just to have an old piece of a car?"

"Aw, Harvey ain't too bright. You know that."

"All right. All right," she said in her singsongy voice, and she got out of her rocker and walked without limping into the house. She just couldn't help preaching to him. And she had him. He didn't want to get into any more trouble. That night down at the police station, when she had to come get him in a taxi, he could have died. She went and talked to the judge whose wife knew her from her beauty parlor days, and Donald never did have to go to court. That's when she laid down the law. He wasn't going to hurt her again, but what she didn't know about Ester wouldn't hurt her. After all.

He worked afternoons the next week as a bagboy at the Hometown for tips, and Old Man Boudreaux gave him a basketful of dented cans of food, which he rolled back to Mamaw's and stacked up on the back porch. She was tickled to death and asked if he thanked Mr. Boudreaux. "Sure, Mamaw," he said and rattled the basket back through the alley to the store.

Old Man Boudreaux had said, "You bring my basket right back as soon as you unload all that good food. Hot tamales, Boston baked beans. Hominy. That's a hunnert dollars' worth of good food, and that basket cost me plenty. Bring it right back as soon as you unload it."

Saturday morning Mamaw shook him awake before good daylight. She seemed to be shaking the newspaper at him. "Son! Son! Wake up! It's your little lady. She died! Look here in the deaths." She couldn't stop shaking him.

"Mamaw! Stop it! Who's dead?" But it was sinking in.

"Look here," Mamaw cried.

He took the paper over to the window and the faint light. There it was, the last in the list of deaths, Mrs. Richard (Ruth) Ward, at her residence . . . "It says she died Thursday night . . . the funeral's Saturday—this afternoon." He lowered the paper, and it separated and fell apart around his bare feet. "Goddam . . ."

"Donald!" gasped his grandmother. He sat down heavily on

the bed, and she gathered up the mess of paper and left him, murmuring, "Poor little thing. It says she was only fifty-eight." She meant the little old lady. She meant Mrs. Ward. Damn. He couldn't believe it.

In the kitchen, Mamaw made coffee for them. He pulled on his jeans, and they sat and passed the stirring spoon between them. Mamaw was quiet except for the muddled little slurping sounds of coffee as she drank. Donald gulped his down and walked through the little house, front porch to back porch. Finally, he came back to the kitchen. "Well, it just means I have to find another job."

"They were such good Christian folks," she said, like it had just dawned on her for the first time. "I felt so safe with you there on Saturdays when all these other wild young'uns were running the streets." She pushed her chair back and took their cups to the old yellowed sink. When she turned on the water, the pipe wobbled from the hole in the floor, some of Donald's plumbing she'd carried on over like he was a master plumber. "Maybe Mr. Ward will . . ."

"No," said Donald. "No he won't. That yard was hers. He didn't care about any of it, the pool or the lilies. Or the goldfish. The honeysuckle will have it in a month." He rubbed the back of his neck. "I'll find another job."

His grandmother smoothed her gray hair back with both hands to the little bun full of hairpins on her neck. She sighed. "How about cleaning up our yard, today. Do you feel like it?"

"Sure," said Donald. And he worked till one o'clock weeding and pruning and raking till his grandmother came out on the porch and said, "Why Donald, you've become a real gardener." He smiled at her. It was no big job. Not like working for Mrs. Ward, with her list of "priorities" for the whole summer. He looked up at Mamaw, frail but straight as an arrow, standing in the door. She came into the yard.

He wiped his damp forehead on his sleeve and shoved the tools under the back steps. "It's hard to believe she's dead. She was all the time complaining, but I didn't know she was really sick. She was all the time saying what all she used to do but she couldn't do anything anymore."

"The paper said folks could contribute to the heart fund," said Mamaw. "Heart trouble. That was it. My mama had a bad heart, and one day she just dropped." Mamaw slapped her hands like a gunshot. "Like that."

"She must've been going down. She didn't stay out long last week. But I didn't think . . . I've gotten so I know what needs doing. I have the place looking . . ."

"I think we ought to go to the funeral."

"Mamaw!"

"I don't know why not. Knight's is right down there on President Street. We can walk!"

"I can't believe you are talking like that, Mamaw. Going to that white funeral parlor. Blacks don't go there. That place is strictly white."

"Of course they do! Jeff Turnage works there. He told me black friends come in to pay their respects at the wake and come to the funerals, too."

"This ain't no wake. They waked her last night."

Mamaw turned to walk up the steps slowly, holding onto the rail. "Well, I'm going. Mrs. Ward was good to you. She kept you off the street and paid you well for it. She taught you about flowers. Now, you can come or you can stay." She paused on the porch. "If you come, put on your good pants and your good jacket and your dark tie. Don't you put on that tie with the jaguar or whatever you call it on it."

"I'm not going, Mamaw." He followed her up the steps and headed for a shower.

At three o'clock when his grandmother came out in her white church dress and hat, carrying her white pocketbook and her palmetto fan, Donald was sitting in the swing dressed like she had told him, his long legs sprawled out in front of him, a hand gripping each chain.

"My, don't you look fine. Now that's what I call nice. Oh, so nice, Son." Donald didn't know whether Mamaw was crafty or not, but she was awful hard to get around. He got up and left the swing bouncing on its chains.

He helped her down the wood steps. And they walked out the gate and down Boudreaux Alley toward President Street. He was wondering if Mamaw really ought to try to walk eight or ten blocks, when Harvey pulled alongside them in his big rusty Chrysler. He smiled his big smile showing the brown and broken teeth that made Donald look away. "Take y'all somewhere, Brother?"

Mamaw smiled gratefully at Harvey and up at Donald's face. "Now, isn't this nice? Thank you, Harvey." Donald was untwisting the wire that held the back door shut. He helped Mamaw in and sat beside her.

"Thanks, Har . . . Brother. We're going to the funeral. It's at Knight's."

"Y'all going to Knight's?"

"That's what I said. Did you hear about Mrs. Ward dying?"

"What you talking about, man? You mean she's dead? What in the world happened?"

"Heart attack, we think. Remember she was all time saying she couldn't do any work anymore. We read it in the paper this morning."

"Aw, man. She was a good lady. A Christian. That's too bad, man." Donald could see that Harvey was really sorry about the old lady.

"You got a job yet?"

"I got a little job, cleaning up at the Paramount at night after the show. Minima. Don't work like I did at contracting. Just a few hours. That's all."

"How you going to make your car payment?"

"Trust in the Lord. He'll take care of me."

Donald didn't say anything to that. They rode in silence till Harvey pulled up at the curb in front of the big white columned building. "Well, here we are," said Donald, working to get the door unwired. "Thank you, Harvey," said Mamaw. "Your car is so nice. You're going to make it, Son. Just trust in Jesus."

"That's it. Yes, ma'am. I do." They stood on the curb, and the car lurched and the tires screeched as Harvey pulled into traffic.

Donald and his grandmother walked on a strip of carpet to the funeral home entrance. Donald wished he had not come as he opened the door and they walked into an ornate vestibule. "Now isn't this nice?" said Mamaw, looking up at the big crystal chandelier and down at the deep rose carpet. "Just look at those fine wooden walls. This must be the finest place in Ste. Marie."

A poker-faced man in a dark suit came toward them like he was on wheels. "May I help you?" Like hell, thought Donald.

"We uh . . ."

"Mrs. Ward," said Mamaw politely, solemnly.

"That's Chapel C, right down this hall."

Mamaw took Donald's arm and they entered Chapel C. The carpet was a deeper shade of rose, and before he was ready for it there was her coffin down at the end of the aisle. He swallowed hard as Mamaw led him right down the aisle with people dressed up, sitting on either side and standing down in front talking like it was a special kind of party. Some organ music was playing in the back somewhere. He just wished he could cut and run, but that was impossible. He began to see the flowers all over the place, baskets and sprays, every color. And on top of her coffin, what were they? Waterlilies! How? It was like they were floating on top of ferns, not Boston, another—that leatherleaf she was so crazy about.

On the fern lay big shiny lily pads, and somehow the stems of the lilies were made to stick up like they did in her pool, the deep yellow one, two of the pink ones, only one of the little blue ones, and several of the whites. He felt a momentary resentment, imagining someone getting over into their pool, his and hers, and cutting out every bloom. She'd said cutting the lily pads made the flowers bloom better, but he'd never known her to cut a lily.

Mr. Ward was standing near him now. When Donald turned to look at him the old man got tears in his eyes and couldn't speak. Somehow it surprised Donald. He'd never imagined Mr. Ward looking any way but distant and kind of cold. He had on a dark blue suit. Mamaw shook hands with Mr. Ward, and he turned like he would introduce them to two young couples back in an alcove where people were talking to them, but then he shrugged as if to say he couldn't get their attention. Donald wondered which was the boy who had made the pool with her and put their initials in the bottom. It didn't matter.

"I appreciate your coming, Donald," said Mr. Ward, "and thank you . . ." Donald realized Mr. Ward didn't know Mamaw's name. That didn't seem to matter either.

"We just wanted to pay our respects, Mr. Ward," said Mamaw in a formal voice Donald had never heard before. The old man got out his handkerchief and turned his back and walked toward the group in the alcove. "We've paid our respects, now, Mamaw. Let's go. Okay?"

"All right, son." And she took his arm and he slowly walked her back up the aisle. People turned to look at them, the only blacks in the little chapel for whites, and some of them nodded politely and smiled just right. Donald had a kind of strange comfortable feeling he didn't quite understand. He did feel sure that he and Mamaw looked as nice as any of the people there. Somehow that did matter. He looked down at the dark rose carpet. It was the color of those little early summer straggly bushes in the side bed, spi . . . spirea. Every week, almost, she'd say, "The pink spirea is still blooming, Donald. I believe it's lasting longer this year than I've ever seen it." They must have those waterlily stems in some kind of water tubes and wires in the stems, and something was keeping the petals open. He looked back down the aisle once more and there they stood upright and alert, like little soldiers prevailing through this strange party for her.

"We should have ridden the bus, Mamaw," he said as they walked out in the bright sunshine.

"No. I can't step up those high steps, and they start off before I can sit down."

"Well, they're air-conditioned." His leather shoes felt tight, and his feet burned.

"We'll soon be home. Don't you want to set our supper out tonight, Donald?"

"Sure. What do we have?" He forced his long legs to take short slow steps.

"Well, we have the gumbo left from last night. Or there's still that cold chicken and those good tomatoes."

"How about some of that canned stuff Old Man Boudreaux gave us?"

"Oh, no. We'll save that for winter."

"Let's have the gumbo."

"You're a good boy, Donald." She was tired, and her voice sounded kind of settled down in her throat, like when she was in the hospital with her hip operation. She leaned more heavily on him. He felt a sudden panic in the pit of his stomach. That could be Mamaw lying in a coffin, not a fine coffin, not in a place like that, but in the Holiness Church, a dead little husk, boxed up and lost to him forever. He looked down on her crisp crinkly gray hair smoothed back to the bun, and his panic turned to something more comfortable. Love. Yes, he loved Mamaw. He loved Ester, too, but that was different. As they turned into Boudreaux Alley in sight of their house, he leaned over and gently but swiftly picked her up in his arms, cradling her like a baby.

"Donald, what on earth. Put me down. Put me down right now. What is the matter with you?"

"Hush, Mamaw, I'm going to carry you the rest of the way. You've walked too much today." When he reached the porch he stood her on her feet and kept his arm around her till she was steady. "Now, you go in and take off all your finery and come out here and sit on the porch till suppertime and we'll have us some gumbo and rice and crackers. And iced tea," he called from inside the house.

"Well, I declare." She smiled and followed him in.

That night as they sat eating at the kitchen table, talking about how good the chicken and sausage and fresh okra were in the gumbo, the phone rang. Donald got up and answered it in the front room.

"Who was it?" said Mamaw when he came back and sat down.

"You ain't going to believe it. It was Mr. Ward. He wants me to come work for him all next week, help him in the yard and in the house, too. Says he has a lot of cleaning out to do."

"Now you see . . . folks just have to keep on going."

"Says he wants me to keep on in the yard. Has a lot of things he wants to get rid of."

"That's always the way—her clothes, things like that."

"I told him I'd be ready Monday morning. I'm kind of worried about our waterlilies. Somebody must have cut them up pretty bad to make that big bunch on top of her . . ."

"Oh, but weren't they beautiful! I never saw anything like them. Just beautiful!" Mamaw's eyes shone as she patted her mouth with the paper napkin.

"Yeah," said Donald, "they're going to need some fertilizer pellets if they're going to come back and bloom again before frost."

Crab Celestine

NICOLE OPENED HER eyes and looked across the white windowsill level with her bed. She lay on her stomach, her cheek sunk in her pillow. I am one-eyed, she thought. This is how it is when you're one-eyed. At first, she saw only the pollen-glazed screen. Then she saw the pecan trees and the little green dogwood that their next-door neighbor, Mrs. Greeley, was so proud of when it bloomed in the spring. She lay still, letting her consciousness quicken, spreading her toes as she felt the cool damp breath of early morning air seeping through the thin cotton of her pajamas and on her feet and ankles.

Then she remembered getting home last night from New Orleans with Mama and Daddy. It had been fun. They had eaten lunch at Charbonnet's, and while Daddy tended to business she and Mama had shopped.

Suddenly Nicole sat up. The red sandals. Mama had bought her the most beautiful and different pair of sandals, red with buckles on the toes and at the ankles and shiny black leather soles. Nicole jumped out of bed and ran over to the dresser. There they were, still in the shoe box, black tissue paper fluffed around them. She took one shoe out and smelled the new leather before she dropped it back in the box.

In the bathroom she got into the tub and out as fast as she could. This was Wednesday, Celestine's day, and if she hurried she could go up and help her bring the clothes back. She dried hastily, leaving the big white towel lying on the floor with her pajamas.

In her room she dressed in her pink-striped seersucker play-

suit with the zipper up the front. Then she sat on the floor and
buckled the red sandals on her bare feet. When she stood up
they felt different from the way they had seemed in the store
in New Orleans, when she had had on socks and walked up
and down on the carpet. Now the red straps cut hard across
her feet and the black soles were stiff. She clomped into the
bathroom and looked at her feet in the mirror. The sandals
were beautiful. I will wear them, she thought. No matter how
much they hurt.

"Nicole!"

Nicole ran noisily to the back porch. "Yes'm?"

Her mother was down in the backyard spraying roses. She
had on her old blue chambray dress with the long sleeves, a
wide-brimmed leghorn hat, and old cotton garden gloves that
were twice too big for her.

"I'm glad you're up early," her mother called. "I left your
chocolate on the stove. And some grits and toast already
buttered in the warming closet. Oh! Do you have on your new
sandals? Come on out and let me see."

On the back steps Nicole kicked one foot up.

"Oh, sweetheart! They're just adorable on you." She
pushed the brim of her hat back off her face with the dark
blue wrist of her glove. It was like she was framed in a big
yellow moon. "I'll finish that little plaid sundress to go with
them. I only have to hem it and work the buttonholes."

"Well, when, Mama?"

"Today, I hope. After I finish this and clean up." She lowered
her voice. "Just look at that blackspot trying to move in on
my Mareschal Neal. I can't have that. It's simply not as hardy
as these good old red and pink radiances. Not as fragrant,
either." She went on talking, more to herself, pumping her
little Flit gun, wetting the rose leaves, while Nicole went into
the kitchen and poured her cup of chocolate, skimming off
the wrinkled skin on top. The grits had a deep crack and she
dipped down to the bottom of the bowl to a pool of butter and
chopped it all up good and ate a few bites with the toast.

Nothing was really warm. She raked most of it into the slop bucket behind the door. Let the hens have it.

"Mama," she called out the kitchen window, "if the milk hasn't come yet, I'm going to ride with René to deliver up to Joyce's in niggertown and walk back with Celestine when she brings the clothes."

"Nicole Foster! What have I told you about that! Now, if you want to be punished good and proper, just let me hear you say that again. Would you like to miss the serial Saturday afternoon?"

"I'm sorry. 'Coloredtown, coloredtown, coloredtown.' Mama, everybody says . . ."

"That'll do, Nicole. I don't mind you riding with René. But do come on back with Celestine. She ought to be bringing the clothes early. We haven't had any rain this week. She's going to stay and make me some pies."

"Goodie." Nicole ran up the hall and out the front door. Her new sandals clopped sharply on the porch floor, and she sat down on the steps to wait for René. The flower beds along the walk still had some dew on them. Except for a few purple larkspurs, all the flowers were pink—sweet williams, carnation pinks, and snapdragons—Mama's favorite color in flowers. Nicole's too. When she grew up she was going to have flower beds just like these. She rubbed out a gnat on her knee. But she was also going to be a good cook. Mama didn't like cooking. She did it when she had to, but she didn't like it. She said she didn't like it.

In the fridge she kept a few cans of pear halves and asparagus and freestone peach halves, and when she had to fix supper, she'd compress her lips and say, well, I know what we'll have for salad, and she'd open one of the cans and lay one of the things on a lettuce leaf and add some mayonnaise and maybe grated cheese. She said she wasn't interested in ever learning one more recipe, that Myrt was good at everything. But on Wednesdays Myrt stayed home and cleaned up her own house and went to early prayer meeting.

There was René stopping over at Dr. Harris's. That meant he'd be at their house next. René Benoit and his brother delivered milk for their daddy. René drove in the mornings and Jacques at night. Nicole loved their car. It was an old Chevrolet two-door sedan that they'd taken the doors off of, and they'd taken the backseat out and put in a big box with a block of ice in it. There was no glass in the back windows, and the Benoit boys could reach from most any direction into the box for bottles of milk or cream or buttermilk or even chocolate milk. They stacked empty bottles behind the icebox. About halfway through their route, they would drive two miles back out to their farm and refill the box and unload the empties. Nicole was sitting there on the front steps thinking of the white buttermilk moustache on her Daddy's upper lip when René stopped in front of the house.

She grabbed an empty quart bottle from the step and was waiting for him at the end of the walk. "René! René! Can I ride with you?"

"What'd your mama say?"

"She said I could."

"Okay. Give me that bottle and take this quart to the refrigerator for me. Hurry up, now. I'm running a little late."

Nicole took the milk in and put it next to the icing unit of the Kelvinator. As soon as she was sure the door was latched, she raced back and jumped onto the threadbare seat, avoiding the coiled springs that poked through. "Can I shift?"

"Okay. But do it like I showed you." He wobbled the stick between them from side to side. "It's in neutral now. When I put my foot on the clutch, pull it back toward me. Not you. Me. Watch out when you go to high; wait till I press down on the clutch again."

"I know."

"Well, you nearly stripped my gears last time." When he pressed his foot down on the clutch, Nicole carefully put the gear in low, and they eased on around the big water oak, heading toward Mrs. Greeley's.

"Where're you going to get off?"

"At Joyce's Grocery. I'm going to walk back with Celestine when she brings the clothes." The boxes of empties rattled behind them.

"Who's Celestine?"

"Our washerwoman."

"Oh." He put his foot back on the clutch, and Nicole pushed the knob through the H motion to high. "That's the ticket. Is that that old yellow nigger? Makes pies? I see her in people's kitchens. She must make a mean pie to be hired just for that."

"You shouldn't say 'nigger.' Say 'colored.'"

"'Scuse me. You and Mrs. Roosevelt. She's got 'em on the brain."

René stopped and put the gear in neutral and pulled up the hand brake. He walked rapidly across the street with a quart of milk for Mrs. Cohen, and Nicole carried a pint of cream in to Mrs. Greeley's refrigerator. Back, waiting in the milk car she saw Mrs. Cohen's fox terrier come flying after René, barking like crazy. René stopped suddenly and threw up his arms at the dog and yelled ahg-g-g at him. The dog ran back and sat on the front steps, barking and shifting his front paws like he'd just love to get his teeth into René's ankle, but knew better.

Nicole and René laughed as he drove on up the street to Joyce's Grocery for colored people.

"Okay, kiddo. I'll take this batch in to Joyce, and you go on to see your washerwoman. What's her name again?"

"Celestine. Bye, René. Thanks for the buggy ride."

René smiled, his white teeth flashing in his tanned face. He hoisted a box of milk to his shoulder, cream golden in the necks of the bottles, and in the tops round cardboard stoppers with a little brown cow and *Benoit's Dairy* printed on them.

Nicole walked along the gravel street toward Celestine's house, swinging her arms, stopping to kick the rocks and sand out of her sandals. She waved and spoke to women working in their flowers or sitting on their porches. They were too old to go out to work anymore, and they got to stay at home while the rest of the family went out and took jobs.

Celestine's house, the worst house on the street, was unpainted, screenless, and had sagging hinged boards on the windows. It sat on wood blocks. Her fence was of dry gray pickets that had been patched with scraps of orange crates and rusty wire. Bricks leaned on each other like dominoes to border the front bed where some tenant had once grown flowers—hydrangeas, maybe, or cannas. There were no lard and coffee cans of snow-on-the-mountain or princess feather on her porch, and this was one way Celestine was different from her neighbors.

There was no grass in the front yard. The earth looked hard and smooth as stone, though Celestine's chickens seemed to find it worthwhile to peck constantly at it, la-la-ing to themselves, like Myrt humming as she worked around the house. Nicole walked through the hens unnoticed, but a big red rooster raised his head and looked at her, fleshy red wattles trembling under his yellow beak. He turned his head from side to side to see her, first with one eye and then the other. His black tail feathers arched, iridescent green in the sun. Nicole watched her step; she didn't want to get chicken droppings on her new shoes.

Celestine was at her business of laundering in the backyard. Her propped-up clotheslines were empty except for the freshly ironed dresses and blouses on hangers at one end. Near the well on the porch sat a big oval willow basket half-filled with stacks of ironed underclothes. Beside the basket was a battered aluminum saucepan of boiled starch. The skin on top reminded Nicole of her breakfast cocoa.

Celestine stood barefoot at her ironing board, a discarded table leaf laid across the backs of two straight chairs. The board was wrapped in many layers of old sheets and tablecloths, the top layer with some badly scorched spots from her hot flatirons. She was ironing thick white bath towels, and she didn't speak.

"Hey, Celestine."

Celestine didn't seem to notice her.

"You about through with the clothes?"

"You in some kind of a big hurry?" Celestine half-turned. "Well, look at them fancy shoes! Where'd they come from, Miss Priss?" She banged the heavy iron down on the board and pressed back and forth on a big white towel.

"We went to New Orleans yesterday. Celestine, why in the world do you iron towels? That seems like the dumbest thing I ever heard of."

"Ax you mama. She says they's too hard dried in the wind. She likes the way they smells, she says, but she don't like the way they feels. Thinks they're going to scratch your hide, I guess." She turned and shook her head sharply to one side, dislodging a long ash from the cigarette she had flattened in the corner of her mouth. Celestine liked tobacco; she also had some snuff between her gum and her lower lip. She tipped her head upward and inhaled a couple of times, then exhaled through her nose as she folded the towel lengthwise and ran the iron over it again. She began a stack of towels on a newspaper on the porch, then she took her iron over and exchanged it for a hotter one that sat in the edge of ashes under her black iron wash pot.

Celestine was heavy and leaned from side to side as she padded around the yard on her strong big feet. She wore a wrinkled dress of many faded colors, and a gray apron with pockets to her knees. She had her cigarettes in a breast pocket placed well above her large sagging breasts. Three kitchen matches stuck in her plaited hair. She flapped out another bath towel and laid it across her board and then made the iron sizzle by slapping at it with spit on her finger. She tested the bottom on a waxy piece of Octagon Soap wrapper.

"How many towels do you have to go?" said Nicole, sitting

down on the plank steps of the little back porch, careful of splinters.

"Oh, less than a dozen, by now, I reckon. I don't count 'em. Don't get paid by the each. What did y'all do in the City 'sides buy them red shoes? That's a new sunsuit, ain't it?"

"It's not a sunsuit. It's a playsuit. Size ten. It's old."

"I ain't never seen it."

"You have, too. We ate at Charbonnet's. You should have seen the fried soft-shell crabs I had. Two. That's all I ever want in New Orleans. Soft-shell crabs. Those big old claws are the best things you ever put in your mouth." She sucked saliva noisily. "Did you ever have one, Celestine?"

"Humph," Celestine spat. "Have I ever had a soft-shell crab? Don't you know I was born in New Orleans? I was cooking in restaurants down there when I wasn't much older than you. I can't hardly believe you didn't know that. I was thirty years old time I moved up here. Shoot." Smoke clouded her face.

"You cooked at Charbonnet's?"

"I didn't say that. I cooked at other places down there in the quarters. I was learning to be a real seafood cook with that chef, then one day that old Isaiah, he come in there, told me a lot of lies, talked me into coming up here. Rode the train up here and stayed. Except for the time I went up to Chicago to see my sister who lives up there."

"What happened to Isaiah?"

Celestine flipped the tiny butt of her cigarette away. "You tell me. He left for somewhere and never come back. And I'm glad to tell you that."

"Charbonnet's is my favorite restaurant in all the world." Nicole leaned back against the post. "Well, I haven't been anywhere but New Orleans and Jackson and Nashville, but Charbonnet's is wonderful." She watched Celestine lumber toward her with two towels to stack on the porch.

"Charbonnet's is all white. White tile walls higher than your head. The floor is little tiny white bathroom tiles. The tablecloths are all white, two of them on every table. The waiters wear black suits, but they have big white aprons over their suits. They can carry round trays of I don't know how many plates piled up with crabs and shrimp and oysters and fish, trays this wide." She stretched her arms as wide as she could. She went on. "The napkins are white and the dishes are white. Big heavy white dishes. Thick gumbo cups— that's what we always start with. My crabs have to be on a platter they're so huge. Well, I guess you know how the crabs look if you've cooked them. But Charbonnet's are golden, not brown, golden, and crisp, and the huge claws stick out at you and just crack off when you pull them the least little bit. They have tartar sauce and french-fried potatoes that are pretty good if you like them thick, and coleslaw in little round bowls. And french bread all over the tablecloth, and they keep bringing more pats of butter the minute you start giving out."

"Yeah, I know all about that. All them restaurants is alike. Place where I was working when Isaiah got me, way down on Decatur, they named their fried crab 'Crab Celestine.' Had that printed on the menu. You oughta seen *my* claws if you want to see some claws." She set her iron on its end and turned to spit snuff-dark juice toward the fence. A hen pecked at the dusty little puddle. Celestine began ironing again. "I was going places down there. I never should of left all that. I know all about them fine restaurants. But I tell you something else, too."

"What?"

"Some of them black cooks spits on white folks's food."

Nicole jumped up, and the pullet near the steps fluttered to one side, its round eye showing alarm. "That's not the truth. Nobody's going to do that. Why would anybody do that?"

Celestine laughed. "Oh, yeah. Yeah, they do it. Some of them. They don't like white people. I seen them do it."

Nicole sat back down and began to lick her finger and polish the dust off her shiny black soles. "Aw, I know they don't do that at Charbonnet's. Mr. Charbonnet would fire them. My daddy knows him." She thought of the crispness of the hot crab batter and couldn't keep out the image of a glob of foamy white, dripping, hidden under the big claw. Frown lines formed between her blond eyebrows. Cooks at Charbonnet's didn't do that. Celestine was just trying to be hateful. Sometimes she was like that. She stuck her fingers in the pie filling to taste it. Nicole had seen her do it in their kitchen at home. Fingers dripping all the way to her mouth and back in the mixing bowl.

"You're just trying to tease me, Celestine. You know good and well no cook does that at Charbonnet's. You probably worked at some old hole-in-the-wall where they hired crazy people. Did you ever spit in food you were cooking? You put your fingers in the pie filling. I've seen you do it. I ought to tell Mama."

"Tell her what you want to." Celestine grunted as she set her iron near the fire and picked up the hot one with a folded rag. Back at the ironing board she said, "I didn't say all cooks do it. I just said *some.* If they're in a good humor and don't have nothing special against white folks that day, they ain't likely to do it. Just forget I said it." She turned and looked at Nicole. "Wipe that frown off your face. It'll grow there for good."

She reached into her pocket and got a pack of Picayunes. She shook a cigarette up, pulled it out with her lips, and pushed the pack back into her pocket before she took a match from her hair. She struck it on one of the rough chairs and lighted up, drawing deeply before saying anything. Nicole was watching her closely.

"Tell your mama she ought to let me do her sheets and pillowcases and your daddy's shirts. They presses wrinkles into flatgoods up at that expensive steam laundry. Worse than that, they presses them sharp creases in shirt sleeves. Ain't no excuse in that. You won't find no line ironed up a sleeve on my ironing board, not as long as I got the strength to roll up a towel and stuff it in there. That is trashy ironing, them creases. Sticking up there like a cane knife. I'm surprised at your mama letting him wear them like that, particular as she is."

"Which would you rather be, a washerwoman or a cook?"

"Ain't no restaurants up here. None except that Moreau's Café, and he does his own cooking. Hmph! I bet that's something. This here's my last towel." She reached into the big corrugated box by the ironing board. "I got a lot to tote. I may have to get you to help me a little bit."

"I don't mind." Nicole wondered how Celestine would manage without her. She looked around the small yard with its crazy fence tied and tacked and patched together. It kept the chickens in and other people's dogs out. Almost everybody up here had at least one dog, ribby, long-tailed hounds and mixes that lay under porches or even in the graveled street, stretched out like they were dead. But they didn't come nosing about in Celestine's yard. Actually Judge Landry's yard. It was hard to understand why somebody like Judge Landry would want to own a place like this. The privy leaned into a back corner, weeds clinging to its sides. In the other corner was a shed with two walls. It held a few tools, a hoe, and a shovel. Celestine had some garden rows running between the privy and the shed, behind low unstaked chicken wire. The okra was blooming, a pale hibiscus, and the tomato plants had little yellow flowers and tomatoes no bigger than chinaberries. The mustard greens were full of bug holes and had turned yellow. They matched Celestine's wrinkled skin.

"If we had restaurants, would you want to be a cook? Couldn't you make more money? You could fix up your place."

"Fix up my place! This ain't none of mine. Don't you know who owns this place? That fine rich judge. He's supposed to keep up the fence and the flue and everything else. The rent sounds cheap, five dollars a month, but it ain't no cheaper

than it ought to be. Wind comes right through the walls in the
winter. What we need up here is some sewages and lights."
When she had ironed and folded her last towel, she walked
over and put it on the edge of the floor. "Okay, let me go back
here a minute, and we'll get this wash down to your mama."

Celestine went back to the privy and opened the door,
scraping the dark earth. She squeezed herself inside and
dragged the door closed. Nicole imagined her lifting the
flowered dress and settling herself on a round hole, flies and
wasps beneath her.

Nicole unbuckled her red sandals and took them off, slapping the soles against each other; then she buckled their ankle straps together. She was disappointed that the shoes were
so stiff; it would be terrible if her feet could never get used to
them before she outgrew them.

Celestine came rocking back and began taking her ironing
board down. She leaned it against the porch wall, next to the
washboard, then carried both chairs into the house. Pulling a
large rag from one of her apron pockets, she tied it around her
head. "I gotta leave my coals alive 'cause I have to pick up
Mrs. LeBlanc's wash after I finish with them pies." She looked
at the clear midmorning sky. "Ain't no rain up there for a
while. Come on."

She lifted a small stack of Nicole's father's BVDs and some
cotton petticoats and dinner napkins and laid them on the
paper. Everything smelled so good and clean. Nicole looked
across Celestine's backyard, with its rotten wood and chicken
mess, and buried her face in the sweet-smelling clothes. She
slung her red sandal straps over her shoulder and lifted up the
stack of clothes, resting her chin in ruffled batiste. "Mmm-m,
Celestine, they smell so good."

Celestine poured water from the long galvanized well
bucket into a basin and dipped her hands into it and patted
her face. She stepped down and poured the water in the chickens' water trough, and slipped her feet into straw slides that
sat by the steps.

"I gets 'em clean." She filled the big basket, finally laying a clean white flour sack over everything, tucking its edges into the sides of the basket. Then she lifted the basket by both ends and hefted it atop her head. She stood only a second or two getting it balanced, then, walking tall and straight, she stepped over to the clothesline, where the hanging clothes waited. She lifted a dozen garments easily, and as she and Nicole walked out toward the street, she swung the dresses and blouses around her left shoulder and held them there.

Nicole ran ahead and lifted the wire loop that held the gate to the fence, and Celestine sailed through, dropping her right arm to her side, no break in her rhythmical strides. Nicole fastened the gate and ran after her.

"Don't leave that gate open. I don't want any of them dogs getting in and stirring up my hens."

"I closed it good. If you come back and it's open, somebody else has been in there."

"Ain't nobody else coming." She started up the street.

Nicole walked carefully along the path that ran in front of the Negroes' cottages, a shallow ditch filled with elephant ears, paper plants, and weeds separating her from the street. The packed earth felt cool and good to her feet. Grass and little wildflowers leaned over the path, and some long grass caught between her toes and stripped little black seeds off on her feet. For two blocks she bounded and danced along, sometimes getting ahead of Celestine, who continued to glide through the street beyond the growth. Sometimes all Nicole could see was the basket floating along like no one was under it.

Past Joyce's Grocery they went up some steps at the corner and made their way on the paved walk toward Nicole's house. They passed under the cow oak on the Greeleys' vacant lot, and Nicole saw a huge acorn that would have made a fine pipe, but she couldn't stoop to pick it up with her arms full. She kicked it to one side and hurried to keep up with Celestine.

Mama met them at the back door and took the hangers from Celestine. Celestine took the basket off her head and set it on the breakfast table. She removed her white cover and folded it over the basket's side.

"Well," said Mama, smiling. She had bathed and put on a nice dress and smelled like soap. "It's not ten o'clock, Celestine. I'm glad you're early. I'm counting on those pecan pies." She left to hang up the dresses, and Nicole followed with her stack. She meant to hurry back and watch Celestine in the kitchen.

"Mama, Celestine wants to do our sheets and Daddy's shirts." She spoke low.

"Oh, she does, does she? Well, why doesn't she tell me?" She closed her closet door firmly. "I want to keep things the way they are."

"But she says the steam laundry presses wrinkles in the sheets and tablecloths and that they do Daddy's shirts wrong."

"Nicole?" Her mother looked at her and frowned.

"Well, I'm just telling you, Mama. And she needs to earn some more money. Her house . . . do you know how poor she is? You ought to go up there . . ."

"Nicole, for pity's sake! I know Celestine is poor. I pay her for what I need her to do. Other people hire her for special work. You may not know it, but Celestine doesn't have the world's best disposition. Sometimes she is almost impudent."

"Yes, ma'am." Nicole started out of the room.

"But you have a good heart, honey. And that's important."

"Yes'm."

When Nicole went back into the kitchen, Celestine had stepped out of her straw slides and was standing at the porcelain-topped table in the middle of the room. She had all the ingredients ready to make piecrust—the big wood flour bowl out of the barrel, the Snow Drift, salt. She didn't measure anything, just threw it all together and added a little water and mixed it with her fingers. She separated the dough into two balls and threw one onto the floured board, patted it flat, and rubbed flour on the rolling pin. She rolled it back and forth, in a way like she ironed, but faster, lighter. She floured her hands again and lifted the thin raw pastry and laid it over a greased pie pan. Then she did it all over again with the second ball for the other pie pan and shoved both pans out of the way like they didn't matter anymore.

Nicole watched Celestine crack her eggs in the big yellow mixing bowl, then quick as a wink add brown sugar, dark Karo syrup, vanilla, then three handfuls of pecans. She stirred it all up good and ladled it out into the pie shells. At first the pecans went to the bottom; then they came to the surface, evenly distributed and coated with the golden mixture that would make them sweet as they toasted on top of the pie.

Celestine continued to work fast. She ran a paring knife around the edges of the crust, trimming them neatly. The oven was already making the kitchen hot. Nicole climbed onto the stool by Celestine's table.

"Well, Miss Priss, I hope you noticed I didn't put my finger in the filling. No telling how it'll turn out without me tasting. I know you came back to watch and see, so you could tattle to your mama."

"I did not. I came back to see that you didn't spit in it."

"What!" Celestine dropped her arms to her sides and drew herself up like a soldier. "Of course I didn't. You know better than that. Those were city cooks I was talking about, bad folks. I never would do that. Don't you mention that to your mama and daddy." Celestine shook her head. "You want to make these chicken tracks?"

"Yeah," said Nicole. "Give me the fork." Leaning farther over the table she took the old kitchen fork and carefully pressed the tines into the pastry, making a delicate pattern of ridges all around the rims of both pies. "How's that?" she said.

"That's fine," said Celestine.

Mama came to the kitchen door as Celestine was finishing the cleaning up. "Good gracious, Celestine, you work fast. If you'll set them in the oven for me, I can take them out. I know you have to pick up Miss Marie's wash and get it into your wash pot in time to hang it out to dry this afternoon. I guess you wouldn't have time to come back and fry some sacolait for our supper." She looked at Celestine. "Mrs. Harris brought us ten beauties a while ago, all cleaned. If you'll come back and fry six for us, I'll give you four."

"Can you let me have a little lard to take home and fry mine?"

"I reckon so. You can take it with you tonight. We might have some Kentucky Wonders left over, too. Myrt has a way of cooking enough for an army on Tuesdays."

"What time you all like to eat?"

"We usually eat about six."

"I think I can make that. I need my hangers."

"They are in your basket," said Mama.

Celestine stepped back into her straw slides. She took her rag off her head and mopped her face with it and dropped it in her pocket. After she washed her hands at the sink she opened the oven door and slid the pie pans in, one after the other. Snapping the oven door to, she said, "If I's you, I'd check these pies ever five minutes after they cooked about forty minutes. Don't let them pretty crusts burn."

"We'll watch them, won't we, Nicole." Mama handed Celestine some dollar bills rolled up. Then she gave her two quarters. "For the pies," she smiled. "I'll give you some change tonight as well as the fish and lard."

"Yes'm, thank you. I'll be here by five."

"Bye, Celestine," said Nicole.

"Bye." Celestine walked toward the back door, carrying her big basket.

After she had gone, Mama turned to Nicole. "She's expensive, but she's worth it. We'll have a treat for Daddy tonight. He adores sacolait. Celestine's even better with fish than she is pies. Knows exactly how hot to get the grease, and how to season the cornmeal."

"She used to be a restaurant cook in New Orleans," said Nicole.

"For pity's sake. I never knew that. Well, no wonder she knows all the tricks."

"She probably would have been a chef at Charbonnet's or Arnaud's by now if she'd stayed down there. Did you know Isaiah?"

"Isaiah? I remember old Uncle Isaiah who used to cut my crape myrtles back every fall. I believe he trimmed the privets, too. But I'm pretty sure he's been dead for years. Why?"

"Oh, Celestine knew him or something. I don't know."

Mama picked up the sandals from the porch table. "I see you came back carrying them." She was sympathetic. "They'll pinch you a little now, but just wear them a while everyday with your socks, and before you know it you'll be perfectly comfortable in them." She held one sandal and forced the shiny black leather sole to bend. "See there? You try it."

Nicole took the other shoe in both her hands and bent it slightly. "I don't want to crack it."

Her mother laughed. "You aren't going to crack it. This is fine leather. Go on. Bend it back and forth some more. Like this. Oh, there's the phone." And she walked toward the telephone under the stairs in the hall.

Nicole stood on the porch slowly folding and unfolding the soles of the new red sandals, her eyes staring unfocused into the pecan trees thick at the back of the yard, smelling the sweet rich pies and thinking of the heat in the big kitchen, summer and winter. She laid the shoe on the table and tried to imagine the high whining music of cold wind whistling through Celestine's old house up in coloredtown, and it became a blend in her mind with the terrifying winter night siren on Sweet Bay's red firetruck flying past their house, under the streetlight and its pretty fluted-plate shade, going

to put out a fire in coloredtown. And the next day driving up
to see a little square of ashes no bigger than Mama's kitchen,
with an old chimney standing useless and bleak in cold
daylight; their houses never burned in summertime. And
Mama's missionary society collecting worn-out clothes and
cans of hominy and baked beans and a bag of flour and meal
for the burned-out Negroes.

"That was Mrs. Greeley, darling. She is going to pin up my
hem for me, bless her heart. I'll be back in a few minutes.
Hook the screen after me." Nicole did not look at her mother,
who would have her new skirt folded over her arm, a pin-
cushion in her hand as she crossed the backyard and walked
through the wisteria trellis into Mrs. Greeley's yard.

Nicole went to the phone in the hall and took out the thin
phone book. Her heart beat a little faster as she turned to
Middleton, which had nearly nine pages to Sweet Bay's four.
Her finger slid down the column of M's. Middleton Palace
Theater, Middleton Seed and Feed, Middleton Steam Laundry. She lifted the receiver for the long-distance call. "Two
four seven in Middleton," she said to Central.

To the strange man's voice she said, "Don't pick up Mrs.
Foster's laundry in Sweet Bay anymore." She dropped the receiver reaching to hang it on the hook, and she heard the
man's voice saying "Hello?" while it swung and turned. As
she hung it up she knew the strange man would call Mama
back and Mama would wonder what in the world. There was
no way she would not get caught.

Her knees felt a little shaky walking back to the porch. She
looked out at the privet hedge behind the rose bed. Its long
switches arched out, keen switches, switching switches,
stripped to one little leaf on the tip. *March out there and get
me a keen switch, young lady.* Mama didn't punish often, but
Mama could be hard, raise long red welts on legs, with her
keen switch. Instinctively Nicole drew one knee across the
other to fend off the stinging swipe.

She took a deep breath and smelled the pies. Mama must

have forgotten the pies when she went off to get her hem pinned up. Nicole could see Mrs. Greeley, old, sitting on the floor, pins in her mouth, yardstick on end, measuring inches from the floor and saying to Mama every now and then, "Turn," the line of shiny pins slowly lengthening like a fine line of ants around the bottom of the skirt.

She took two dishrags folded up thick and opened the oven door a crack. A slither of sweet searing heat struck her face, and briefly she saw the pies, pecans glistening over shaky filling, the pretty crusts beginning to tan. She shut the hot door. She took the alarm clock to the porch and sat down with it in front of her to watch. She would check the pies every five minutes. She would not let them burn.

Quicksand

SO. COME IN, Frederick. You're late.

I've been wondering when you would get home. Howard Colson called me, your little henchman of a doctor. Cancer, my eye! Do you really think I'm such a fool that I would fall for that play on my sympathy? Will you never learn? What do you expect to gain by such a heartless subterfuge? What do I have left that you can claw off of me, squeeze out of me, other than my imperishable dignity and goodwill? And you'll never get that. What are you up to now? What are you setting me up for? It doesn't matter. What have I to lose that I really want? My wheelchair? My isolation? My nurses? Pills? Placebos, probably.

You have me cornered. Treed. But I'm not done for. I'm too smart for you. That is my ace in the hole. I've always been smarter than you, and I'll die smarter than you. Cancer! That you would stoop to corrupt the noble profession of medicine—the healing arts—with bribery. It's a new low. But how many doctors have you paid to provide false reports to suit you? How many psychiatrists? How many of these witch doctors have you paid and paid and paid to say I'm crazy. All those absurd terms and phrases—schizophrenia, paranoia! What do you know of Freud, Jung, Adler? What do you know about the arts—music, literature, the great painters? Nothing. You haven't read a book since you graduated from college. All you know now is what I tell you. Without me you would be nothing.

All you know is power through money. I am your prisoner, all through your money. And your meanness. How many lawyers have you bought off just when they were ready to slap my divorce papers on you? Trapped, treed, I am. But never without my wits. No. I will always be ahead of you. Waiting there at the finish line like the tortoise. Laughing there in the briarpatch like Brer Rabbit. Money cannot purchase intellect, Frederick.

I guess you are going to say my smoking gave you cancer of the lung. That sounds like something you would dream up. Leave me with a killing load of guilt. Is that your intent? I killed you. I'm a murderer. But you're not going anywhere. You don't have lung cancer. And if you did, don't you know I'd have it first? I'm the smoker. I'm the inhaler. I'm the goat. The goat, the goat, the goat! Baa. Baa-aa. Baa-aa. Take your hands off this wheelchair. HELP! HELP! HELP!

Louella! Yes, yes, I need you. What do I pay you for? It's time for my pills. Quick! While he's in the pantry. Give me two! Do as I tell you! I'll fire you on the spot. Two! I'll have you jailed. Please, please, Louella!

Thank you. Now hand me that water.

A martini! That's your answer to everything. I wonder what you would look like without a glass in your hand. You'd probably lose your balance and fall flat on your face. Like one of those movie star posters fallen over in a theater lobby. I suppose your alcoholism is the greatest grief you have burdened me with. For thirty-five years. Thirty-five years.

Thirty-five years. Drunk. You're a drunk. And you wanted to be a father. A father! What a travesty that would have been. But my judgment prevailed. I knew I could never bear to have a child whose father was you. What a bizarre idea. What a gross baggage of bad genes and unspeakable environment you might have wished upon a poor, innocent babe. A poor little boy destined to emerge from his cherubic infancy to traipse right down in your terrible footsteps. Or a beautiful little girl to cower before your horrifying browbeating. Tyranny! An innocent, innocent dainty little blonde, blue-eyed girl in my image to be served up to some vile male out there in the terrifying expanse of this world's depravity. Sacrifice to another foul appetite. My daughter! I won't have it! I won't have it!

I wouldn't have it.

Don't touch this chair!

Alcohol fiend! Sex-maddened viper! What I've lived with. And for so long. So lonely. No friends. All my friends, gone. Ladies, happy women with decent husbands, all gone. All gone. Repelled by your disgusting person. You've ruined my life. Ruined, do you hear me! A psychological reign of terror staged relentlessly against my peace of mind. Oh, the toll on my frail body.

You haven't seen my body for twenty years. You'll never see it again, either, never touch me again! Don't look at me like that. Look away! Look away! I know you! I know what you'd do if you could. Even now. Why have you come in here and upset me with your lies. The only creative thing you know how to do, lie. Your only art. Louella! Louella! Come and roll me to the elevator. I'm exhausted. I'll have to have a sleeping pill. You see what he has done to me. You're my witness! But of course you've been his varlet for decades. You're bought and paid for just as much as your ancestors were. Little difference.

Cancer! Frederick, you don't have cancer. I've had enough of this cruel charade. I am willing to forget this. Forgive and forget. The story of my life. I cannot deal with you. Hush! I'll write you a letter tonight and have the morning nurse put it by your plate at breakfast. Louella, are you coming, or will I have to make this chair go by myself.

Dear Frederick, You know how I love you. I cannot help my-self. I am a loving person. You can never know the slavish agony of my devotion to you. I forgive you for everything. But no more cruel jokes, my love. I did not sleep all night. It is now 5 A.M. and Marion has come on. I hope I can sleep now and all day up here in my silken cocoon. Have a lovely day at the bank. I'll be dressed in my finest for you tonight. I'll wear my diamond necklace. We will celebrate! Your faithful Lila. P.S., Give my regards to your son when he comes in today. I know he's yours.

So. Come in, Frederick.

Come in! What on earth is wrong with you? You're absolutely gray! Have you been drinking already? Before five? Couldn't you wait till you got home? Slinking into some darkened backstreet tavern with the riffraff. Heaven knows we have enough liquor here for an army. If I had the money you spend on alcohol to spend on my wardrobe, I'd be the best-dressed woman in town. The truth is I am already. I'd be wearing chinchilla. But who in this town knows chinchilla from rabbit. I can just see you buying chinchilla for me. If you are buying chinchilla, I have a good idea who you are buying it for.

Did you have a lovely day? Tell me about your day, Frederick. Tell me how it feels to come home in the afternoon and have a caring person say, How was your day? How does it feel, Frederick? I wouldn't know, of course.

What is this?

What is this? For me! What are you up to, Frederick? Beware of Greeks. Wha . . . my goodness! What a . . . a . . . what a large stone. Well it is large, isn't it? It's far too large—massive—for a hand as small as mine—not what you'd call blue-white, doesn't exactly "shoot fire." It must be four carats. Five! Well. It's very . . . interesting. Thank you, Frederick.

Where did you get it? Did you order it from Tiffany's? Did you buy it off a tout at the track for a pittance? Is it something your mistress threw back in your face? I do not trust you one inch, Frederick. I cannot afford to trust you. You have lied and cheated me too many times. I am alert to you. Don't ever forget that. Where did you get it? How long have you had it?

Did she wear it for a month? A year? Five years? Twenty years? Did he bring it to you for her? Did he say, "Here's something Mother asked me to give you, sir?" Does he call you sir? When the two of you are alone does he call you Father? Dad? What a mess you've created. You and your craven appetites.

All right. All right. It doesn't matter. What good does it do for me to weep and wail? What chance do women have? Ladies? I surely cannot let you think you've put this over on me. I knew twenty-five years ago you were carrying on with her, and I've seen him! He looks just like you. Any fool could see that.

So you had your way with that little strumpet. I can just imagine. Ugh! The senior warden and his strumpet! The civic leader and his bastard son all set up beside him in business. Do you think I won't contest your will? One red cent to that boy and I'll blow that will sky high. You won't be here to pay off the lawyers, the judge. I'll no longer be your victim. I will have come into my own. Out from under your Fascist thumb. I'll be renewed, fresh, ready for the fray. Jeanne d'Arc in shining armor. The Maid of Orleans. But I shall not be burned at the stake. I'll rise from this wheelchair, fling off my shackles . . .

That's right. Walk out on me. Rude! I must remind you, you were reared better than that. At least they taught you some manners. Leave that pantry door open so you can hear me! Ice rattler! Befouler of my Baccarat! I'm sure you're drinking more in there than you are in here in my presence. You don't fool me, Frederick. Not for a minute. I haven't forgotten what it was like to be the wife of a perfect gentleman. Edward! Oh, I never mention him to you, but he was a gentle person, from the soles of his long elegant feet to the top of his head, I'll tell you. And handsome, too. Of course, he had two things in common with you. He drank, and he was MALE. He too had ideas. Babies. Babies! Between the two of you my body would be ruined now. I couldn't stand him. It's sickening. I never open my mouth about him to you, of course. But I'll tell you something that sets my teeth on edge. He went back to California, and his second wife and he had six children. Lived on a ranch! Imagine. He was no moneymaker, so I can't think how he could afford such a family. It's disgusting. Reproducing like farm animals. Edward was a city man! A ranch indeed.

I'll have to hand it to you, Frederick. You can make money. I wouldn't want to hear just how you've managed to make so much. I've always wondered who you're cheating at that bank. Widows! Orphans! If the authorities ever come after you, I can certainly plead innocent to any knowledge of your nefarious dealings. Don't expect me to lie for you. I was reared to tell the truth. Greed and falsehood are two deadly sins that have never tempted me.

Did the boy come in today? What is his name? What did you name him, Frederick? Roger? Did Roger come in today? Back you go, another martini! Drunk, drunk, drunk. You can hear me! I saw him. I saw him when you had the unmitigated gall to include him in the secret office party you sneaked in here Christmas when you thought I'd retired upstairs. (You did not invite me!) Oh your face when that elevator door opened and I rolled out into the hall. It was wonderful! It was rich! There you all were. In my house! In my house! There you were, smiling, making merry, your arm around Roger's shoulder. The fruit of the hussy's womb. The fruit of your insatiable loins.

He even has a streak of your Jewish looks. Oh, I can see it in you, Frederick. Your hair, your coloring. However little Jewish blood one has, it crops up. Your mother told me before we married that her grandmother was one-fourth Jewish. I didn't tell you. I didn't let that stop me. I knew why she told me. Didn't want you to marry a divorcee. Ah, well. Mothers and sons.

What are you holding that vodka bottle at me for? You must have taken leave of your senses. Me? I would never let that

Bolshevik abomination pass my lips. Are you implying that I'm a Communist? Ask Louella if she drank it. She and the others are stealing me blind—trying to get me to walk! Telling me the doctors say I should walk. That I'm able to walk. They want me to fall again. The weaker I am the more they can take advantage of me. And why get up, I ask myself. You'll just knock me down again and break more bones. Isn't that true, Frederick? Isn't it? It doesn't matter. We both know what you are capable of. It's no use. Wife molester.

It's well known that you struck me, knocked me down, and crippled me for life. Everybody knows all your unpardonable sins against me. Not that I've ever revealed my shame to a soul. I'd never open my mouth on such a shameful subject. People know I'm a lady, Frederick, a gentlewoman. Blue blood flows through my family's veins. We are not materialists. We're quality. Our heritage is just something you've never known, so you can't appreciate what it does for one. You're ordinary, Frederick. Common. Part Catholic, part Jew; like a lot of Episcopalians. Like a puppy with enough guile to end up in a chic pet store instead of the pound. And I married you because you were making money and it looked like you might make more. I was divorced, temporarily at outs with my relatives, and I had to deal with the vulgar threat of poverty. I was still too young to know not to rush into another marriage. So we were married. Thirty-five years ago. Thirty-five years. And you are too insensitive to comprehend the unslacking hell it has been for me.

Men are so awful. Loathsome. Animals. Just awful. Get away from me! Don't ever come near me again. I'll call the sheriff. Do you own him? I'm sure you do.

My daddy used to take us for long rides in the country on Sunday afternoons. Frederick, sit down! You need to hear this. My mother would lead us from the front seat, and we'd sing "In the Gloaming" and "Drink to Me Only with Thine Eyes," and all the Stephen Foster songs. It was a genteel way of life. Our values were fine. So fine. We were ladies and gentlemen. We'd ride along in our big car on the nice crunchy gravel roads, rumbling across wooden bridges over the clear swift creeks, singing, the shade of forest oaks and sweetgums and magnolias dappling the red clay, birds darting at odd angles in front of the car. We were all dressed beautifully. We stayed dressed beautifully all the time. We didn't slouch around the way people do now. We were quality, Frederick. We never thought our perfect lives were going to end. Mine faltered when I married Edward. It ended when I married you. I detest you, Frederick. You have mongrel blood in your veins, and your mother had to get married. Sit down! Don't run to that bar! Listen to the truth. It has found you out, Frederick. To all intents and purposes you are a bastard, almost as much as your Roger. Stop it! True to me? Ha! You deny that bastard? Everyone knows the truth. Everyone in this miserable little town you have trapped me in.

"I've never loved any other woman but you, Lila!" Don't make me mock you. Mockery doesn't become me. Of course you don't love me. A man doesn't strike the woman he loves. No! When a man mistreats a small defenseless woman, he doesn't come crawling to her with untrue tales of being mortally ill just to get her pity. A man doesn't do that, Frederick.

Don't touch this chair!

Who was that on the telephone?

Houston! Are you expecting me to believe you have to go to Houston, Texas, for treatment? Is that what you want me to believe? What a perfect plot. You and that criminal doctor are setting me up for you to have a plush two weeks somewhere with that slut. So that's what that tasteless jewelry was setting me up for. Damn you, Frederick! You just cannot accept my superiority. You may think you are going to run off with that woman, but you're not. I'll tell you you are not. Houston, indeed.

You're so selfish, Frederick. Only the purest selfishness could make you pull a trick like this. A mean, horrid trick. Louella! Bring my pills. I'm ready to go up!

Good night, Frederick. Lou-ella!

Darling Frederick, Your breakfast note: I'm willing to forget whatever you did last night. Let's just start today anew—a clean slate. You know that I love you too much to let a little spat mar our enduring relationship. Have a lovely day. See you tonight. Ever your Lila.

So. Come in, Frederick.

Why are you coming in with that smile? You do look seedy tonight. Please don't put your jacket on my best chair. Your crony called me this afternoon. He hung up in my face, the crass blatherskite. More rubbish about going to Houston. Says he's accompanying you to see a surgeon he knows. Really, Frederick, isn't this carrying your prank a bit far? Need you cook up so elaborate a ruse? Enough is enough. Let's just forget all about it. I bear no ill feelings. Notice my earrings. The ones you bought for me in Lucerne in 1960. The same day we got my watch at Bucherer's. That was the trip when we had an audience with Pope John, wasn't it? Remember my dress? Truly the most beautiful black dress I ever owned. And the most expensive. The other women looked like cooks compared to me. A drab lot, I must say.

Remember the jeweled sheath I wore to the Paris Opera? Absolutely unforgettable with my full-length mink. Now, wouldn't I have been tacky in that old fingertip ranch? And the divine suit I wore that night at dinner in Rome. Oh, I get all these trips abroad mixed up. Of course, I'd like to forget Ireland, staying in that castle owned by some Texan you knew. It was awful—drafty; he had a rotten cook. Thank heaven I'd ordered those crates of Waterford before we got to the castle. Did you really think I could exist in that place for a week? In one day and out the next. I'll have to say you managed the return passage to the States in a hurry.

Ireland was a bore. What did you like about it? For that matter, what did you like about Florence? Why would someone who knows nothing about art want to get out and walk and walk and walk the streets of Florence? You never heard of the Uffizi or the Pitti until I told you about them.

Shopping in Tokyo and Hong Kong was a lark. I've never unpacked half the things we bought in the Orient. But those people are dirty little things. Their food makes me ill to think about it. Oh, but we've literally been everywhere and done everything, haven't we?

I'm going to Houston with you, Frederick. I will summon the strength. Remember the man picked up his piano when the house caught on fire. He carried it right out the front door. A mystical surge of strength comes to us in times of great stress. If you're lying to me, you'll not have your assignation. If you really are ill, you need your wife beside you. Your helpmeet. Hand me my ivory cigarette holder. This onyx one is worthless. My lighter, please. When are we leaving?

Tomorrow! Are you mad? You can't expect me to be ready by eight o'clock in the morning! Nobody goes anywhere that time of day. I'll require four or five days. I'm not your servant, you know, to be ordered about. Not your chattel no matter what you might think. I'll have to go to the beauty parlor. I need a massage. My clothes aren't ready. Louella! Go up and get out my luggage. I'm going to Houston with Mr. Frederick. Now you can stop nagging me to get out of this chair, you and those blackguard doctors, those charlatans. Well, I'll get out. I'll get out and I'll go to Houston. We'll see who will outsmart whom. Louella, roll me to the elevator. You need a haircut yourself, Frederick.

Don't tell me I "can't go"! I knew it! You don't want me along. I'll bet you don't. I'll just bet you don't. I told that doctor I was onto your tricks. The cur slammed the phone down in my face. Thirty-five years. Thirty-five wasted years. A life wasted on an alcoholic. A sex deviant. I've always suspected it. If that boy isn't your son, what is he to you, always hanging around, so young and handsome? How old? Twenty-three? Twenty-four? You think this elegant sweet little lady doesn't know about worldly aberrations? You think I'm dumb, stupid. Oh, no! I'm not dumb. Don't forget one very important fact: I have read everything. There isn't much I don't know. Ask me anything. You don't know enough to ask an intellectual question. It's you who's stupid, Frederick. Oh, how stupid you are. You and your bank. You couldn't add two and two without a machine to do it for you.

You and your adoring employees. My God, Frederick, are you too stupid to know why they adore you? Because you ply them with bonuses and gifts and extra holidays and tickets to the races. And wild parties, I'm sure. They're stupid nobodys just like you, Frederick. Stupid and rotten. Rotten to the core, my fine husband.

I'll tell you something else your mother told me, sir. She was pregnant with you before your father married her. It was the worst kind of disgrace in those days and you know it. She had to get married. That adored father you worshipped so was trapped. Victim of the oldest, most rancid little game in the whole world.

Frederick! All right, go on! Hit me! Strike me! Strike me! Brute! Rotter! Wife beater! Go on! Go on! You've done it before! Do it again, Frederick.

I am not shouting!

Coward. You know better than to hit me. Touch one hair on my head, and I'll take a bottleful of sleeping pills. This time I'll succeed. I'll take them while you're in Houston, at night, while no one is there to see. Remember that. They'll call you at your hospital or at your love nest, wherever you are. Your wife is dead, Mr. Brent. She had been dead for hours when they found her. You haven't forgotten, have you? The night you threatened to have me put away. I showed you I meant business, didn't I? Didn't I?

Why didn't you let me die? How far can you carry cruelty? Why can't you buy me a cottage on the rocky coast of Maine? Give me two faithful servants, some good books—everything on Edward and Wallis, the *Titanic,* the Galveston hurricane of 1900—a meager income for food, shelter, the barest amenities, and you'll never hear from me again. Oh, don't look so hangdog, Frederick. My needs are so little. And for denying me you will answer to God, Frederick. Your behavior does not go unnoticed by your Maker. You will rot in the hell of your own making, Frederick. Light my cigarette, please.

Are you standing there trying to tell me that you are going to Houston in the morning with that wretched Howard Colson? I cannot believe this. What is your hurry? Frederick, are you mad? I'm serious.

Don't touch this chair!

Get out of my way. Louella! Take me to the elevator.

One last thing, Frederick. Don't bother to get a haircut. Your hair will all fall out soon. Did you know that? If you are telling me the truth. It will fall out by the handful. Louella!

Dearest Frederick, good morning. Whatever was said between us last night, whatever little unpleasantness, let's forget it, shall we? After all, we only live once. In my opinion we should put aside childish differences and enjoy each other.

I'll expect you home in time for tea this afternoon. You can even bring Howard with you, that naughty doctor. He never comes to see me anymore. I'll wear my white linen with the Belgian lace, and my emeralds you bought me in Rio. We'll have a merry old time talking, just we three. All my love, Lila.

The Authoress

ALL THROUGH THE noisy luncheon Glory Bea would lay her hand over her wine glass when the waiter came patrolling her side of the long table. On his last trip around behind her, she almost relented and left her hand in her lap and let him pour. But she didn't. She held her head high and drank ice water. Even more than *author* did she prize her name in this town as *impeccable lady.* And ladies did not sit around in public restaurants at two o'clock in the afternoon drinking wine.

She had sat there through the annual autumn Junior Fortnightly Club guest luncheon, not reading one of her stories for the program for the first time in ten years, listening to that overweight Ella Follett, who could not wait to fill in with three vocal selections from *The Sound of Music,* a cappella. Standing up there, lifting her hand, walling her eyes back like a dying cow. Those voice lessons her mother put her through certainly had made a fool of her.

Glory Bea simply had not been able to write a new story. Everyone in Ste. Marie was highly impressed by her prose. They told her so and praised everything she ever read, extravagantly, even though her *oeuvre* had ended up unpublished and in dress boxes under her bed. She was the only fiction writer in Ste. Marie, Louisiana, near the reedy shores of Lake Pontchartrain.

She leaned back from the white tablecloth and pressed the sides of her neck. With each throb of the artery against her fingertips she was feeling a small terror. It seemed to rise in the mounting noise of voices, the clatter of dishes, cutlery, ice. The smells of food, wine, bodies, were beginning to stifle her. Even the fabric on the arm of the woman seated next to her rasped on the back of her hand as Glory Bea pushed back her chair.

"Excuse me," she murmured, smiling, gracious, somewhat aloof, and walked sedately toward the hall and the sign LADIES.

In the rest room she chose the lefthand booth, which had the new toilet. Sliding the bolt on the door, she groped in her needlepoint handbag. She drew out an elegant perfume flask encased in sterling filigree, a gift proffered on some triumphant occasion to a remote lady, in fact her mother. She quickly unscrewed the polished top and drained the clear contents into her upturned lips. Silent and odorless and comforting, it shot down the clean chute of her perfectly poised throat.

She sat down and patted her lips carefully with a square of tissue, then gently removed a cerise smear from the neck of the flask. For the vodka she sighed a deep and grateful breath. Everything was really all right. She shot the little bolt and stepped out, giving the handsome woman in the mirror a dazzling smile.

"Have you had cosmetic surgery, darling?" she asked, then opened the hall door and returned to the mindless din.

The luncheon was breaking up, and every member and guest who could get to her told her how they missed hearing one of her lovely romances, how disappointed they were— out of earshot of Ella Follett, of course, who was, after all, a charter member of Junior Fortnightly, and Glory Bea was not, quite.

"Let's go," she said to Opal, moving toward the porch of the Ste. Marie Tea Room. But the new Presbyterian minister's wife stopped her.

"Oh, Miss Bolton, I was so looking forward to hearing you read today. I am distressed to learn that you aren't writing lately. I want you to know that Mr. Terry and I are deeply interested in the arts of this community. We want to encourage them in every way we can. Have you ever sent anything to the *Christian Herald*? With a name like Glory Be, you ought to catch their attention!" She reached up and patted Glory Bea's sharp jawbone. "Don't let those old Yankee magazines discourage you, Precious." The tiny woman chimed out a little laugh for herself.

Glory Bea and Opal pushed themselves on through the crowd, the Estée Lauder, raw silk, and Ultrasuede. Outside on Marigny Avenue the Buicks and Continentals and Cadillacs were parked every which way on the roots of live oaks in front of the tea room, but the two women hurried around the corner to walk home, a kind of Mutt and Jeff pair. Opal had grown wide, but Glory Bea remained a beanpole.

They walked silently, intently, careful not to trip over the uneven sidewalk jutting up over persistent roots that plowed through and under the whole town. They seemed not to notice the gentle drift of Spanish moss hanging from oaks and magnolias, moving on the October breeze off the lake and redolent of salt water and the crab boil that came from exhaust fans at the rear of every little restaurant in town.

"Good Lord," Glory Bea said later, standing at her picket gate. "Now when did any fool ever see a story in the *Christian Herald*, I'd like to know. That preacher won't last long here with an absolute tree frog for a wife." Opal giggled, her face rosy from wine. "And my name isn't Glory Be, she'll learn if she ever does get to hear me read. It's Gloria Beatrice," said Glory Bea, as if Opal hadn't known that for fifty years next month. "If it takes some kind of freak name to catch their attention, if *that's* what they want, they can all do without my work. *McCall's* and *Good Housekeeping* could get down on their knees and beg me, and I wouldn't send them another one of my stories. I'm through with all of them. Fiction in these magazines is trash, t-r-a-s-h." Glory Bea raised her chin high. *When you pass forty, press your tongue against the roof of your mouth to tighten the sag of your throat.* Papa.

"Well, you ought to keep on writing more stories for Ste.

Marie," said Opal, who had been a widow for years and lived three doors down from Glory Bea in a gingerbread cottage choking on fig vine. "I can't see why you don't write about your papa, you all being so close, and him being such an interesting man, if ever I laid my two eyes on one. Why don't you ever write about Mr. J. J.?"

Opal was dumb. Glory Bea had always known it, had tried to tell her that she didn't really know Papa; she just thought she knew him. Nobody knew Papa but Glory Bea. "No, I can't write about Papa, Opal. I've tried. I loved Papa. He raised me right by himself. Did his best, in his own way. He was a lovely man, a gentleman of the old school. A true gentleman of Virginia transplanted to Louisiana. But I have told you, Opal, Papa had a sweet streak and a mean streak, and I found it impossible to maintain my dedication to the purest art of fiction when I tried to write about him. You see, Opal, every time I would start writing about Papa, what was a sweet story, I'd write myself straight into a mean corner with him, and it could be terrible. Then if I just broke down and started a plain flat-out mean story about him, I'd find myself in the midst of the sweetest little tale anybody ever heard of, but by then Papa would have flown the coop. He mixed me up so I just decided to wash my hands of him, in a literary way, I mean. Interesting as he may have been." And this was why Glory Bea could put up with Opal's dumbness. She could speak to her like this, in confidence. Up to a point.

Opal spread her fat little fingers over her mouth. "Well, what do you know, Glory Bea! If you don't beat all. You writers are just something else. I just always thought Mr. J. J. Bolton was terribly, terribly interesting and a perfect gentleman always. He was real witty, too, but sort of remote, too. Romantic! And traveling on a train as a boy all out west and way down into Old Mexico in the days when nobody went way down there. He told me he learned to speak Spanish down there. Mr. J. J. had a mind like a steel trap, and that's the truth."

"I began a story about Papa's travels as a boy one time, one of my early works. I was well into it when I sat down with him and asked him how my grandparents could let an eighteen-year-old-boy—that's how old he was—of gentle raising get on a train and be gone a year, and you know what he said? He told me, 'They didn't let me. I just walked down the tracks to Fayetteville and caught the night freight.' "

"Freight!" gasped Opal, looking up and down John Law Boulevard. She laid her hand comfortingly on Glory Bea's arm. "Maybe he was fibbing, honey." She paused for a moment and looked thoughtful. "Well, couldn't you say—I mean write—that they permitted him to take a tour and let him travel by daycoach? Like that. Then you could write about him working with Mexicans and all. And learning to speak Spanish. It would be grand at the fall meeting next year. I let the committee talk me into being program chairman, Glory Bea . . ."

"Oh, Opal, I never heard Papa use but one phrase in Spanish. I heard him say it many times till I was old enough to look it up in the Spanish-English dictionary."

"Let me guess."

Glory Bea smiled down at Opal. "All right, guess."

"Mañana?"

"Guess again."

"Adios?"

Oh, no, Opal. My goodness, those are just words everybody knows."

"I give up," said Opal, cheerfully.

"Besa mi culo."

"What? What does that mean, Glory Bea?"

"Look it up," said Glory Bea, wishing she had never brought it up. Why had she? She was going too far, letting Opal in too far.

"I don't have a Spanish dictionary. I took French."

"I know. It means . . . 'Let's shake hands.' "

"Oh, how genteel! That's just like Mr. J. J.! I've never known one line of Spanish. I can't wait to spring it on somebody."

"No, Opal," said Glory Bea. "I wouldn't do that. Its vowels have to be pronounced just right. Anyway, it's pretentious to go around spouting foreign terms. Show-offy. Don't do it." She sighed. "As for whom or what I shall next write about, if the muse strikes again, I'll find other subjects." She sighed again. "Being an authoress is not all peaches and cream, Opal. People are jealous of success, you know. You wouldn't believe what I go through with. Mavis Gumm always smiles at me and says, 'Well, here comes our big celebrity.' Just like that, as mean as an old alley cat. I know what she's up to."

"Maybe she just . . . well, that's just poor Mavis' way."

"Poor Mavis, my foot." Glory Bea gripped the sharp point of a picket. "I ought to write a story about 'poor Mavis.' I'd never write myself into a sweet corner with her. I could stay on the mean streak straight as an arrow to the last word."

Opal grabbed Glory Bea's hand. "Oh, Glory Bea, why don't you?" Then she let go. "But you'd have to disguise her mighty good, or I couldn't use you at the autumn guest luncheon next year. I mean not with Mavis sitting right there, recording secretary."

Glory Bea went kind of limp. "Opal, believe me, I am suffering from writer's block."

Opal looked alarmed. "My dear! I had no idea!"

"Writer's block is not gastritis or sinus, Opal. I just mean the well has run dry. I find nothing to inspire creativity anymore. I'm just . . . blah."

"Why Glory Bea, how can you say there's no inspiration living in this lovely town in the bounty of our beauties of nature? Just look at the way those magnolia limbs sweep the ground right there in your own yard. If I could write like you do, I'd write a romance novel about that tree." Opal looked like she had just struck oil in her backyard. "Two lovers could meet there in the moonlight. You could write about the scent of the white blossoms, and the moonlight reflecting on the glossy leaves, a tall handsome man and a beautiful young girl

in an ivory gown with Chantilly lace and drop shoulders."
Opal stopped for breath and rolled her eyes. "They could
stroll hand-in-hand under the trees along the Bogue Kanokee
under the moss and all."

"There you are," said Glory Bea, her mouth in a thin line.
"You be the writer. Go home and write it, and you can read at
the fall meeting. You can do your own program."

"Glory Bea! Are you serious? Do you honestly think I could
write a story? Like you?"

"Well now, Opal, be realistic. Remember I've been at it for
years . . ." This was getting boresome.

"Would you read it for me, what I put down, and tell me if
you think it's good?"

"I'll find time to critique it for you," said Glory Bea. "I'll
tell you something else. Mrs. Landrieux over at Reymond is
looking for a program for the Climbers' Club's May meeting."

Opal forgot herself and squealed, "I could wear my blue
Ultrasuede and my dyed-to-match blouse. Oh, I'm going
home right this minute and start," she giggled "before the
muse stops striking or I get the writer's block." She grabbed
Glory Bea's hand. "Oh, thank you, Glory Bea. Ste. Marie's
own laureate!" Her six gold antique bracelets clattered
toward her elbow as she waved good-bye.

Glory Bea strolled to her house, where she had lived alone
since her papa had died ten years ago. On the porch she gazed
back at the magnolia tree, idly. The foliage did glisten darkly.
There was darkness in the depths of its shade, even in mid-
afternoon. A small smile began to pick at one corner of her
mouth.

By the time she reached her bedroom, she had her earrings
off. Papa had thrown a fit when she had her ears pierced on her
thirty-fifth birthday. They tinkled in a glass box. She put her
purse on the purse shelf in her closet and her shoes on the
shoe rack. Closing the door she leaned back on it and looked
around the room, at her lace panels, her rose carpet, her hand-
crocheted counterpane, the sepia photograph of Papa on the

wall over her desk. "Well, here we are, Papa," she said, looking away from his eyes.

She sat down at her desk, where, along with some bills and a cup of pencils and pens, there lay an open lined pad. Pristine. Ready. Glory Bea selected a sharpened pencil. She tapped the eraser against her chin a few times, and then she began to write. Slowly: *Angelica Pryne . . .* no, she scratched out *Pryne. Angelica Davidson, a gracious southern lady, still young in spirit, though mature in the qualities that count— judgment and taste—strolled out into the starlit grassy lawn. She and her father had just finished their evening repast with a glass of good port from his well-stocked cellar.*

"Ah, my dear," said her handsome father, stroking her long blonde waves with his hand, *"why don't you take a stroll in the cool evening air?"*

"Thank you, Father. What a lovely idea. I'll get my lovely shawl that Aunt Veronica . . ." No, she had used Veronica in "The Rose Beyond the Wall." Damn. She crossed out *Veronica* and continued: *". . . Lucinda crocheted for my sixteenth birthday."*

"Splendid, my dear. And I'll have a pipe in the library. Come in for a goodnight kiss, my child, before you take a chill." He smiled and nodded his leonine headful of wavy white hair. Glory Bea went back and read all she had written; and once again she felt the thrill. Once she got started it was always this way, like a motor racing. She got up, pushing her spindly chair away with the backs of her knees, and went back to the pantry where she poured herself a half tumbler of bourbon. She took two deliberate swallows and felt it hit her scalp. "What the hell," said Gloria Beatrice Bolton, and she went through the house and locked all the outside doors. Then she hurried back to her desk.

Reaching under her blouse she unhooked her brassiere and began to shake the straps loose over her shoulders. She pulled one strap down through one sleeve, then the other. Then she pulled the whole bra from under her blouse. Sitting on the side of her bed she caught her panty hose at the waist and pulled them down over her stomach, buttocks, down her long calfless legs. Rolling back, her legs in the air, she bicycled bare legs a few times and landed on her feet on the floor. "Jesus God, Pappy, I'm glad to get out of that."

Veronica stepped out onto the verandah. Hell's bells; what was her name? Angelica. *Angelica stepped out onto the verandah. A miasmic dampness filled the night air as the beautiful young woman wrapped her shoulders in the lovely shawl that Aunt* . . . Glory Bea took a sip and flipped back for a look at the first page and continued: *Lucinda had knitted for her.*

The moon shone down with a mirrored glow on the dark glossy magnolia leaves, and the soft scent of the blossoms smote her aristocratic nostrils.

"How blessed I am," Angelica murmured. "Here I am, young, beautiful, the daughter of a handsome father, whose granddaddy owned two hundred slaves but freed them all long before the law said he had to. Freed all those sweet soft-singing darkies purely out of his own Christian spiritedness." This was her heritage. "I am fortunate indeed," she reiterated.

Hark! What was that? A sound emerged from under the dense and glowing magnolia boughs.

"Who goes there?" Olivia called, pressing her soft white ringless hand to her soft white bosom, modestly covered with tucks. "I say, who goes there?"

A tall dark man came strolling out from under the tree. Angelica drew back and gasped "Oh!" in surprise.

"Good evening, Miss . . .?" Glory Bea emitted a long bass belch.

"Miss Olivia Pryne." She stepped back a pace toward the verandah.

"I beg your pardon, dear lady. I had no wish to startle you,

*but the rustic bench under yon magnolia beckoned a weary
stranger, and I could not resist to sit a spell and drink in the
splendor of the night."*

"How do you do, Mr. . . . ?"

*"Henry Sampson, ma'am. I'm indeed happy to make your
acquaintance." The tall handsome man walked toward the
beautiful Angelica.* Glory Bea quickly stood up and took off
her skirt and blouse. Sitting back down in her peach satin
slip, she peered down briefly at the bars of ribs disappearing
under the wide, flat ecru lace. She clutched the cut-glass
tumbler and took a noisy swig. Now, let's see, she thought,
he's walking toward me—toward what's-her-name—Olivia.
Oh, God, Angelica! Have I been saying Olivia? I'll get a better name before I read it to the club and send it off. She took
another swallow and laughed out loud. *McCall's* and *Good
Housekeeping?* Besa mi culo. And the same to you, *Christian Advocate.* Glory Bea hurried back to the pantry and
brought the bourbon and set it on the floor by her chair. She
pulled her slip down carefully; the cane seat was scratchy.

She whispered, "I'm rolling now. I'm writing a real love
story, and Papa, you're going to behave yourself this time.
This is a lovely unsullied young lady."

She read back, squinting, seeing double just a bit. *Shut one
eye.* Papa.

*The tall handsome man walked toward the beautiful An-
gelica. "If you can forgive a lonely stranger for being so bold,
you are surely the loveliest flower it has been my privilege to
gaze . . ."* She locked her feet behind the chair legs. The front
door bell rang. Goddamn it.

Glory Bea grabbed up the bourbon and headed for the
bathroom. Then she remembered the doors were locked, so
she calmly sat on the lid of the toilet and beamed at herself in
the mirror. She pulled the loose skin under her chin to the
back of her neck. "You smart little fox, you," she said, teeter-
ing dangerously toward the tub. "Just be still and they'll go
away, whoever it is."

She decided to peek out the bedroom window. It was Opal. Already she was bringing pages of handwritten manuscript. Good God from Vicksburg. That poor pain in the butt. I was too kind to her, thought Glory Bea. I never should have encouraged her. Now she'll be on my tail forever.

The bell rang again. "Oo-hoo, Glory Bea-ee! Gloria Beatrice! Let me in by the hair of your chinny-chin-chin! It's your fellow author! Oo-hoo!"

Oh God, she's walking across the porch to my window. That crazy old coot. Glory Bea flattened herself against the wall.

Opal chirped, "Well, she has just picked up and gone off to the grocery or somewhere. I'll leave her my first page. Won't *she* be surprised!" She rolled up a page and stuck it under the screened door grille.

Glory Bea watched Opal's square flat behind as she walked down the steps and out to the street. "She's always walked like a damn duck," Glory Bea laughed to herself and walked slew-footed back to the bathroom and poured herself a small drink in her pink plastic gargle cup before she went back to her desk.

"*. . . my privilege to gaze upon.*" *Olivia smiled modestly and allowed him to take her small hand in his large manly one, briefly, before she stepped back a pace.*

"*You are very kind, Mr. Davidson,*" *she murmured.*

"*Won't you join me on the rustic bench under your glorious magnolia tree?*" *He waved his arm as gracefully as the wing of an egret toward the dark shadows 'neath the glossy leaves of the magnolia tree.*

"*Oh, I really do not know that I should.*" *Olivia had been raised a perfect lady.*

"*I don't mean to be forward. It's just such a lovely evening.*"

"*Well, I'm sure it is quite acceptable,*" *murmured Olivia. "The hour is early and my dear father is sitting just inside the house, smoking his pipe.*"

The handsome stranger led Olivia to the bench, which, not being extremely long, forced the happy pair to sit in fairly close proximity to each other.

Glory Bea looked back. What in hell did I call him? She found *Henry Sampson* and wrote it on the back of the phone bill. "That'll fix your little red wagon, you sapsucker, you. I won't forget your frigging name again." She went back to the bathroom and poured more bourbon into her cup. She tipped the fifth to one side and laughed. "Not enough to write a novel on, but maybe enough to keep my handsome father from going ugly on me."

She sat down again and picked up her pencil. It was dull now, so she threw it under the bed and pulled a sharp one out of her grandmother's souvenir cup from the St. Louis World's Fair, 1904. Not that poor Granny got to go to the fair. Grandpa went alone, the old bastard, left Granny at home, and brought her a two-bit china mug. Men! She was glad she had never married one. Now she'd just have an old fool, probably some old drone going on sixty, blowing smelly cigar smoke at her air fresheners. She used to think she wanted a husband when she was young. Young dummy. Papa's girl. But now that she had matured, she realized what a nuisance a husband could have become.

She consulted the phone bill and continued: *"Henry Sampson was wearing some elusive yet familiar cologne or shaving lotion—strange—she could not quite place that odor—scent. It didn't smell too good, actually, but the lovely young girl was eager to know this handsome stranger who had dropped into her life like a comet from the star-studded sky. She would tell him about herself, her lonely life with her wonderful father, her dreams . . . She glanced timidly at his profile.*

"Yes, I'm only passing through your lovely town. I am a sales representative for the Meridian General Supply Company. Drug sundries . . ."

"Oh! And what do you sell?"

"Sundries, small drug items."

"Medicines! How splendid. My maternal grandfather was a physician."

"I am very successful, I might add." Mr. Sampson talked to Angelica for an hour about selling in drugstores throughout a large territory in Mississippi and Louisiana. The Mississippi Gulf Coast was his favorite area.

"Oh, how perfectly divine," she said occasionally. She was far too polite and well reared to interrupt and talk about herself, her lonely life with her adored father. Mr. Sampson laid his arm across the back of the bench, allowing some gentle pressure against her shoulders.

Glory Bea left it at that: *shoulders* period, deciding not to mention old Lucinda's shawl again. "I've given that old biddy enough credit for that moth-eaten shawl," she muttered and hiccupped. She brought the bottle back to the desk from the bathroom and set it on the phone bill, careful not to smear *Henry Sampson*. Damned phone bill. Damned phone. Nobody worth a damn ever called. Committee women. Do this, do that. Bored, idle, aging. Like me, thought Gloria Beatrice Bullshit Authoress Bolton. She clutched her pencil. A lump was forming in her throat, pressing hard against her adam's apple, and tears stung the backs of her eyes.

Suddenly the front door opened and Angelica's handsome father stumbled onto the porch. Glory Bea squinted hard at the terrible words. She glanced up at the sepia photograph. Shithead.

"Angelica," he bellowed drunkenly, "where the hell are you? It's getting late, and I want you to get your ass in this house now. Now! Do you hear me?" He swayed, steadying himself on a rocker, as he turned on the porch light. "Where in hell are you, girl?"

Mr. Henry Sampson sat bolt upright. "Who? What?"

"Pay no attention," Angelica tittered, and fluttered her wrist in an offhand manner. "He's our housekeeper's eccentric husband. Thinks he owns the place. Go away, James," she whispered, fearful that her handsome father would hear her.

"My word! Are you sure he is safe, uh, all right?"

Miss Angelica Davidson stood up. "No. I'm not sure. I must call Eglantine. And you better go, Mr. Sampson. I'm sorry, truly I am."

"Well, I say! I am sorry." Henry Sampson began to back out from under the magnolia tree, toward the gate.

"Angie, who the hell is that in the dark out there with you? You got some no-count bum out there?" Her father's shirttail was slipping out of his good country tweeds as he staggered toward Henry Sampson.

"This gentleman is Mr. Henry Sampson, a salesman of drug sundries from Meridian, Mississippi. Do get a hold of yourself, James."

"James?" Olivia's handsome father caught Mr. Henry Sampson by his tie and swung him around in a full circle, unsettling his hair in the dark thick magnolia branches. "Well, you listen to me, Mr. James Rubbersalesman, you get your butt out of here before I cut your corporocity off with a grapefruit knife. Right behind your ears."

Overcome by his own wit, her father turned Mr. Henry loose and fell into a fit of self-applause.

Henry Sampson took off, thoroughly shaken, and was never seen or heard from again by Miss . . . Glory Bea took another drink as she turned back to the first page . . . Angelica Davidson. "Goddamnit. I should have written all these damn names down on the damn phone bill to begin with," she muttered, swinging her head low over the desk, like a pendulum. But she raised her head and shut one eye.

Angelica rushed into the house with her weaving father hard on her heels, his state of inebriation almost too shocking for the young woman's delicate sensibilities.

"Now, honeybunch, don't be cross with Daddy. You know I can't let every Tom, Dick, and Harry come in here and get smart with my Angie."

"But Father, why in God's name did you have to be so crude! If you had just stepped to the door and called me softly, I'd have heeded your summons at once." Glory Bea meant to keep this Angelica sweet no matter what her handsome father pulled, damn his black heart. "But no gentleman is ever going to give me a second look, Father."

"Life just passed right out of her and into you. When you flew out into the world, my little butterfly, she was dead. Everything ended. Your grandfather came for his chrysalis and took her back." He would hug her to him and say something like, "She was an excellent rider, sat her horse like a cloud. That's how we met, you know, a horse show in Charlottesville . . ."

"But I don't want a goddamned rubber salesman crawling in here after dark under my magnolia tree." He smiled at her, one eye closed. "There you are. Now then, let's be friends again, Sweetheart. Have a little nightcap with Daddy. A little bourbon and soda. I know you love that sodapop." He poured three ounces of liquor into a cut-glass tumbler on the tea table and squirted the seltzer at the glass. "Here, Baby, forget that smelly bugger. What the hell was that perfume he was wearing, anyhow?"

Papa used to read to her at night. If she brought fairy-tale books or nursery rhymes, he would laugh and say, "Ah, you don't want to hear that crap." Glory Bea remembered some books he would read—*Black Beauty*, and he would turn two or three pages at a time to hurry it along, thinking she didn't notice. He was crazy about "The Pied Piper of Hamelin," which scared her with all the children following the piper and the nasty rats. He loved "The Cask of Amontillado," but in a thousand readings, he never finished it before falling asleep. Papa was a lot of good things, but to this day it still angered Glory Bea that he thought she was too dense to know when he turned several pages at a time.

Papa was two people. On the rare occasion that a visitor called at their door in the daytime he was courtly, all charm.

At night he never answered the doorbell, and he forbade Glory Bea to.

Angelica did not answer her father. She drank the whole drink down, slowly and steadily, and handed her glass back to her handsome father. He refilled it, then followed the elusive tumbler with the seltzer bottle as though he were stalking a roach with insect spray. Angelica drank half of her drink, solemnly watching her father. Then she giggled. "I know what it was."

"What what was?" Her father's eyelids hung low. His face was red and moist as a toiler in the fields.

"I know what scent he was wearing. Didn't it stink, though?" Angelica laughed and fell back in her chair, and the laugh turned high and shrill. "It's your joke, Papa."

"What joke, Sister? Come on, tell Daddy."

"His cologne was panther piss, Papa, 'pure old panther piss.' Couldn't you tell? Didn't you recognize it? Can't you remember sitting out on the backsteps that day telling me the joke about the lady whose husband gave her a bottle of perfume for her anniversary?" Veronica leaned forward and whispered, "Panther piss. Panther piss, panser pith. Now don't tell me you don't remember that lovely scent." Her slender young form trembled with mirth.

For a moment Angelica Davidson's handsome aristocratic father looked almost sober. He lifted the heavy lids over his curdled eyes and looked serious, like he did when he told her about his grandfather freeing all his slaves when he didn't have to yet. He didn't say anything. He just let out a long wild yell and began the loudest belly laugh Olivia had ever heard come from a human being. "My handsome father has gone stark raving mad," thought Olivia. But then she began to laugh, too. "Darling father, you haven't told me that joke in years," she wailed, laughing and crying at the same time. She got up and stumbled over the footstool, trying to sit on her handsome father's lap. She missed and sat hard on the marble hearth.

Olivia's father stopped laughing as suddenly as he had begun, and he fell out of his chair onto the red carpet. He lay perfectly still on his back, his arms and legs spread out, a black oriental medallion framing his leonine head perfectly.

Glory Beatrice Bolton sniffed and looked at her empty bourbon bottle. "Mean old bastard," she said, moistening her pencil point. *Angelica's handsome father had fainted from fatigue. His loving daughter covered him with the lovely shawl and stepped daintily over his prone form and went to bed with great dignity.* "Simple-minded little slut."

And then when he was old he died one night in the rain beating a mule that had got into the yard and was trampling her mother's old box-bordered rose beds. He ran out with the dustmop, screaming curses at the mule, crashing the shaggy mop over its neck and rump, while the animal stood unmoved, dumb, and wet, glistening in the flashes of lightning. Watching from the dining room window, Glory Bea saw Papa suddenly drop, falling half under the mule, which then threw its hind legs awkwardly into the air and leaped away and was gone.

Glory Bea shrieked and ran out into the storm, believing her father had been struck by lightning. But it had been a massive stroke she was told later. Neighbors and townspeople, whom she usually only saw outside her home, began to wander in casually the next day to have a look at him, laid out splendidly in a fine coffin in front of the fireplace. "A native of Virginia," the paper said, "a resident of Ste. Marie for forty years . . . a revered citizen . . . preceded in death by his wife, the former Gloria Alicia Heyward . . . survived by . . ."

Glory Bea picked up the empty bottle and took a wandering route toward the kitchen. Somewhere she took the wrong turn and found herself in a room she didn't recognize. What? There was Papa's rolltop desk. On the mantel was an enlarged photograph of a young girl jumping her horse over a hurdle, the girl, her hair flying out behind her, and the horse, the two of them suspended there like a cloud. Forever.

I'll follow this fence," she said aloud, holding onto a row of chairbacks, her fingers tracing the curves and arches in the wood. *If you ever get lost, my dear . . .* In the kitchen she put her bottle into three grocery bags and twisted the tops tightly and dropped the bundle into the trash compactor. The bottle popped harshly, then crunched into dust.

The doorbell was ringing. "Ooh hoo. Ooh hoo. Ooh hoo, Glory Bea, it's me! Child, I've written six more pages! Are you in there? I just couldn't wait till tomorrow!" Opal opened the screen door and banged the heavy knocker. "Well, I guess she's still gone. She's not going to believe her eyes!" Glory Bea tried and failed to give Opal a raspberry.

In her room she took up the pad and began to tear pages out. Dully she thought of what she had been writing—nothing she could read to the Junior Fortnightlies. Damn it, if Papa . . . She didn't feel like swearing or drinking anymore. She felt terrible. It must have been the trout amandine at the Ste. Marie.

She lifted one page and squinted close to read the two top lines. "*. . . out of here before I cut your corporocity off with a grapefruit knife. Right behind your ears.*"

Glory Bea fell across her bed in her peach satin slip and tried to breathe shallowly and slowly. Papa had taught her everything she would ever need to know.